Other books by Christine and Christopher Russell

The Quest of the Warrior Sheep

The Warrior SHEEP Go West

CHRISTINE & CHRISTOPHER RUSSELL

EGMONT

This book is dedicated to Kozue san,
a little Warrior from the East.

EGMONT
We bring stories to life

The Warrior Sheep Go West
First published in Great Britain 2011
by Egmont UK Limited
239 Kensington High Street
London W8 6SA

Text copyright © Christine and Christopher Russell 2011

The moral rights of the authors and cover illustrator have been
asserted

ISBN 978 1 4052 4377 3

1 3 5 7 9 10 8 6 4 2

A CIP catalogue record for this title is available from the British
Library

Typeset by Avon DataSet Ltd, Bidford on Avon, Warwickshire
Printed and bound in Great Britain by the CPI Group

Contents

1
Red Tongue

They only went into the barn to get out of the rain. But that just goes to show that big adventures can start when you least expect them.

Sheep, even Rare Breed sheep, don't normally mind getting wet, but it had been pouring for days and the paddock was hoof-deep in mud. Jaycey, the pretty little Jacob, had had enough.

'Ohmygrass . . .' she said, trotting into the cosy barn. 'All this rain. I'm having *such* a bad hair day.'

'Don't be silly, dear,' said Sal, the fat and motherly Southdown ewe, as she followed. 'Only humans have hair. And there's no such thing as a bad *fleece* day.'

'That's right, man,' agreed Links, the large Lincoln Longwool ram, even though his own woolly locks were dangling damply in front of his eyes and he couldn't see where he was going. 'Fleece is cool, innit.'

He bumped into the door-post on his way in.

Wills, the skinny Welsh Balwen lamb, skipped in after Links. He liked the barn. Usually, there was a laptop in there.

Only Oxo, the great Oxford ram, was reluctant to go inside. The rain made the grass grow longer and sweeter. What was there not to like about that? But he was a sheep and sheep stick together, so he tugged up a last juicy mouthful and squeezed in after the rest.

The hens, who lived in the barn, squawked and fluttered for a few minutes then settled again, and the sheep made themselves comfortable on the straw-covered floor. They sat facing the laptop, which was propped on a bale of hay in the middle of the barn. Jaycey and Wills, the smallest, were at the front, with Sal, Oxo and Links behind.

The laptop belonged to Ida White, who owned Eppingham Farm where the Rare Breed sheep lived. She often left it in the barn playing music for the hens. This particular wet spring day she was downloading some new tunes for them, some gentle pieces as a change from their usual pop and rock. The second track was just beginning as the sheep settled down.

Wills, whose mother had died when he was young, had spent his early lambhood with Ida and her grandson, Tod, in the farmhouse kitchen. He had learned a lot about human ways and could even read a little. He slowly read out the words on the screen.

'Sheep May Safely Graze . . . J. S. Bach.'

'What's J. S. Bach?' asked Oxo. 'Something you can graze on?'

Wills shook his head. 'No, I think it's the name of the composer. The man who wrote the music.'

'Shhh,' said Sal. She was gazing happily at the laptop. As the music played, the screen showed a picture of sheep grazing in a beautiful sunlit valley. 'How fortunate we are to be sheep,' she murmured.

'Yeah,' agreed Links. 'But this ain't exactly a banging vibe, is it?' His curls bobbed up and down as he nodded his head, trying to compose a rap. It wasn't easy to make the words fit the slow music.

'We is Ovis Aries, that's our Latin name,

But you can call us sheep cos it means the same . . .'

Jaycey was also peering at the laptop but she wasn't interested in the music or the pictures. She'd noticed her own reflection in the screen and was studying it carefully. Finally, she relaxed. Not a bad hair day after all. And she was massively prettier than any of the safely grazing lot on the screen.

Oxo tried listening to the music for a few seconds but could only hear his own stomachs rumbling, so he gave up and dozed off.

Then it happened.

The sheep on the screen disappeared and, from the blackness that replaced them, a red tongue emerged. It filled the screen, showing the rough, red surface and the tonsils dangling behind. Then came the voice.

'Hi, all you Rams and Ewes and Lambs. This message is for *you*. We're gonna slaughter you. We're on our way. Red Tongue! Remember the name!'

The sheep scrambled to their hooves and looked fearfully around. Oxo marched to the doorway and glared out. The paddock was empty.

The laptop spoke again. 'Red Tongue! Remember the name!' Then the tongue disappeared and the sunlit valley returned.

'Ohmygrass . . .' Jaycey huddled close to Sal. 'What was that?'

4

'I think,' said Wills, 'it was a pop-up.'

'What's a pop-up?' asked Oxo.

'A sort of advertisement,' said Wills, though he didn't really know what an advertisement was.

Oxo lowered his great head and pawed the barn floor with a hoof.

'Just let him pop up again,' he snorted. 'I'll be ready next time.'

Sal raised a hoof for silence.

'Red Tongue . . .? Red Tongue . . .?' She was speaking in the odd voice she used when she was trying to remember something important. 'Yes . . .' she said at last. 'It's there in the Songs of the Fleece!'

'Uh-oh . . .' murmured Links warily.

The Songs of the Fleece were ancient. They had been handed down from ewe to lamb for centuries. Not many sheep knew all 365 verses like Sal did, but most knew a few. Sal looked gravely at her fellow Rare Breeds.

'Verse 204,' she announced. 'One of the prophetic verses.' Then she added for Wills' sake, 'Most of the Songs tell of our glorious history, you see, dear. The prophetic verses tell us what is to come.'

Wills nodded politely. Despite not having had a mother to teach him sheeply things, he knew that much. He glanced at the laptop again. He felt sure he'd heard Ida say pop-ups were a nuisance. They arrived from nowhere then disappeared again. Just like the red tongue had done.

But Sal was clearing her throat so Wills turned to listen.

'A terrible monster will come from the West,' she cried dramatically,

'And a brave flock of Warriors will be put to the test.

For this monster has woken from centuries of sleep,

And its stomach will hunger for sheep. Then more sheep.

Hundreds of thousands will die every hour,

All the sheep in the world it will seek to devour.'

Sal paused for breath but before she could start again, Jaycey's trembling voice had taken up the verse:

'Like a gigantic dog from the West it will come . . .

And the name of this monster, be warned, is: Red Tongue.'

Jaycey looked at them all with frightened eyes. 'My mum taught me that.'

She wobbled on her dainty feet then fainted.

There was silence for a few moments then Links said, 'So. We's done for, is it? We's all gonna be eaten by a monster dog.'

'The Songs of the Fleece are never wrong,' said Sal.

Oxo frowned. 'Yeah, but what was that about Warriors?'

Jaycey opened one eye. 'They'll be put to the test,' she wailed. 'I don't want to be put to the test.'

There was another silence while they all pondered.

'Is it us again, Sal?' asked Wills.

Once before, the little flock of Rare Breed sheep from Eppingham Farm had been called by the Songs of the Fleece to save sheepdom. They had destroyed Lambad the Bad and saved Lord Aries, the mighty Ram of Rams who lives above the clouds.

Sal answered Wills' question by reciting the next two lines:

'Who will come forward in the hour of need?
Hope will lie only with those of Rare Breed.'

Oxo turned towards the doorway.

'Can't be clearer than that,' he said. 'Let's go!'

He charged out.

'Yeah, man,' agreed Links. 'The Eppingham Rare Breeds is the rarest of the rare, innit.'

'We did it once, we *can* do it again,' said Wills bravely.

But then Oxo reappeared.

'So, um, where does this Red Tongue hang out, exactly?' he asked.

Sal thought hard then cleared her throat again.

'To the place where the monster first wakes you must go,

Where the sun scorches fleeces and the hottest winds blow.

But only the bravest will withstand this test.

Remember. Red Tongue . . . will wake in the *West*!'

She dropped her head, briefly overwhelmed by the task facing them. The discomforts and dangers of their first quest came back to her. They came back to all the sheep. Was it really possible to survive and triumph a second time? And where was the *West*, anyway?

Wills ran through the verse in his head. They had to go West, to a place where the hottest winds blow. Not Wales then, he thought. He'd been born in West Wales and didn't remember any hot winds there. No, it had to be somewhere much further away than Wales. He tried to picture the maps in Tod's atlas. West . . . very hot . . . He realised the others were looking at him expectantly and tried to sound more confident than he felt.

'The most likely place,' he announced, 'is America.'

'No problem,' said Oxo, and turned once more towards the barn door.

'Uh, there is actually,' said Wills. 'America's across the sea. How will we get there?'

'We are sheep!' declared Sal. 'Famed as great thinkers. Think, all of you. Think.'

They were thinking so hard, they didn't hear a car drive slowly along the lane and pull up outside the farmhouse.

The smartly dressed driver leaned from the car window and wrinkled his nose.

'Ugh!' he said. 'The country!'

He straightened his tie, picked up his briefcase and stepped out, placing his shiny shoes in the mud. He had an important message for Mrs Ida White.

2
Chilli Soup

Ida White and her grandson Tod were in the kitchen making soup. Ida was actually Tod's great-grandmother and, as he was an orphan, also his guardian. Tod loved living with Gran. She was ancient, older than anyone else in the village of Eppingham, but life with her was never dull. She had taught him to read, ride a horse, mend a bike, feed a motherless lamb, sew and cook. Tod didn't consider himself clever, but he knew a lot for a twelve-year-old.

Cooking the Ida White way wasn't like any other. They didn't bother with recipe books because, as Gran said, where was the fun in knowing how things would turn out?

Tod was standing by the stove now with a bunch of carrots in one hand and a banana in the other.

'What do you think, Gran?' he asked.

Ida looked up from stirring the big soup pot.

'We've got enough carrots,' she said. 'The banana might be good, though. We haven't tried banana before, have we?'

'I don't think so,' said Tod. 'And it should go well with the apple and bacon.'

He sliced up the banana, threw the pieces into the pot and opened the fridge.

'What else?'

He'd just found a handful of chilli peppers when he heard the door knocker.

'I'll go,' he said, wiping his hands on his apron. 'Go easy on the chillies, Gran.'

Gran nodded and dropped two into the pot. She heard Tod open the front door and a voice she didn't recognise. Her mind was no longer on the soup. She dropped in two more chillies. She heard Tod invite the stranger in and close the front door. She dropped in two more.

'Mrs Ida White, I presume?' said the smartly dressed man, coming into the kitchen. 'A pleasure to meet you.'

Gran dropped the last few chillies into the pot and turned to meet their visitor.

'I'm John Smith, and I'm here on behalf of Rhubarb,' the stranger announced.

'Oh, yes?' said Ida politely.

'The Society for Rare, Humble, Unwanted, Beautiful And Rare Breeds?' said Mr Smith. 'RHUBARB for short.' He looked expectantly at Ida. 'They're very big in America?'

Gran shook her head. 'Sorry,' she said. 'I've never heard of them.'

'Ah, but they've heard about *you*,' said Mr Smith. 'And your amazing sheep.'

'They have?' Gran was astonished.

John Smith smiled to himself. This was going to be easy.

'Indeed,' he said. 'And they would *love* to meet them.'

'Any time,' said Gran. 'I'm usually at home.'

'No, no, dear lady. Not here in Eppingham. At the convention. In America.'

Gran didn't know anything about a convention. She sat down. Mr Smith leaned closer.

'Rhubarb want you to exhibit your wonderful flock at their convention centre,' he explained. 'It's a showcase for the talented and beautiful. A sort of Ovine Oscars. And your sheep would be the stars.'

Gran swallowed hard.

'I'm sure that would be wonderful,' she said, 'but I don't think we could afford to . . .'

'No, no,' laughed Mr Smith. 'They would go as the *guests* of Rhubarb.'

'They?'

'The sheep. We'd take great care of them.'

Gran shook her head vigorously. 'Our sheep never go anywhere without us,' she said. 'Do they, Tod?'

Tod was shaking his head too. 'Never.'

'That's absolutely *not* a problem,' said Mr Smith. 'You can go too.'

He snapped open his briefcase and began taking out papers.

'Rhubarb will pay all the expenses. It won't cost you a penny.' He beamed at Gran and clicked his silver ballpoint pen. 'Just sign here.'

He pushed the papers towards her.

'Why?' asked Gran suspiciously.

John Smith laughed. 'Merely to acknowledge receipt of these free first-class airline tickets: for yourselves and your sheep. And free airport transfers and free luxury hotel accommodation.'

He produced a wad of tickets with a flourish and placed them on the table in front of Gran. Tod was tugging her sleeve and whispering.

'Gran . . . I think we should check this out. Where's your laptop? I'll look up Rhubarb.'

Gran nodded.

'Good idea,' she whispered back. 'It's in the barn.'

John Smith heard this and stiffened. Maybe this wasn't going to be such a doddle after all. But his smile didn't falter.

'I can understand this has come as a bit of a shock,' he said, putting himself swiftly between Tod and the back door. 'But Rhubarb are so looking forward to seeing your sheep. And, of course, all the profits go to, er . . . the Lost Lambs Fund.'

Gran blinked. Something else she'd never heard of. John Smith relaxed. All he had to do was work on the old lady's soft heart. And keep the kid away from the laptop.

'A worthwhile cause, I'm sure you'll agree,' he beamed. 'This is your chance to help all those unwanted pet lambs, dumped after every Christmas.'

He held out his silver ballpoint pen. Gran hesitated, then took it. Tod picked up one of the tickets.

'They're for today!' he exclaimed.

'That's right,' said Mr Smith. 'You'll be up and away this very evening.'

Gran looked up at Tod. He shrugged. The tickets seemed real enough. He saw a twinkle in Gran's eye.

'Go for it?' she asked.

Tod grinned. 'Go for it, Gran.'

'Excellent,' said Mr Smith, whisking away the paper as soon as Gran had signed it. 'I'm sure you won't regret your decision.'

He had no idea whether she would regret it or not. It was his job to persuade her to accept the offer and he'd done that. He would get paid. Beyond that, he didn't care. He snapped shut his briefcase.

'Will you stay and have some lunch with us?' asked Gran.

John Smith tried to refuse. He'd done his bit and

now he wanted to wash his hands of the affair. And the smell of the country.

'So kind,' he said, 'but I really must be getting back.'

But Gran wouldn't take no for an answer. Tod cut some bread while she dished up the soup.

Mr Smith took a polite mouthful. His eyes bulged, his nose ran and sweat broke out on his forehead. He swallowed and felt the fiery concoction trickle down his throat and burn corners of his stomach he didn't know existed. He smiled fixedly, loosened his collar and took another sip. By the time he left, he'd removed his jacket, his shirt and his socks.

'What a nice man,' said Gran as she closed the front door. 'He looked a bit hot though. Do you think I overdid the chillies?'

'A bit,' said Tod. 'But the banana was good.'

They stared at each other for a moment.

'Well,' said Gran. 'I'd better go and pack. Though Mr Smith said we won't need much because it's hot where we're going.'

'Where exactly *are* we going?' asked Tod. He picked up the tickets again and shrugged. 'It only says America. Is that normal?'

Gran shrugged. 'I don't know, dear.' Then she did a little jump and punched the air. 'Who cares? America . . . Yipeee!'

'Yipee-iyo!' shouted Tod. He opened the back door. 'I'll make sure the sheep are ready while you're packing.'

'Right,' said Gran. 'And while you're there, you could check out Rhubarb on the laptop. See how big their convention centre is.'

3
Batteries Charged

While Mr Smith was in the farmhouse, smiling and clicking his ballpoint pen, the thinking sheep had had a thought. Well, one of them had.

Wills had remembered that Ida sometimes used the laptop to get things like hen food and fence posts. And he'd wondered if you could use it to get aeroplane tickets to America as well.

So he'd found a stick and carefully tapped some keys: A.M.E.R.I.C.A.–W.E.S.T. The screen beeped and flashed.

'Ohmygrass . . . is it Red Tongue again?' whispered Jaycey as they crowded around the laptop.

The screen went blank and then an aeroplane zoomed across it and more words appeared.

'DESERT AIR,' Wills read aloud. 'THE FASTEST WAY TO THE WEST. WANT TO KNOW MORE?'

'What's desert air?' asked Oxo.

'Deserts are mega-hot places, innit,' Links cried excitedly.

Oxo looked at him doubtfully.

'Trust me,' said Links. 'I know these things.'

Wills had once told him about deserts. Wills knew because he'd seen them on cowboy films. Tod and Wills both loved films about the Wild West.

'But are they places where the sun will scorch fleeces and hot winds blow?' asked Sal.

'Bound to be, innit!'

Links was quivering with excitement. His long curls bounced up and down on his forehead.

'And I suppose,' said Wills, 'that Desert Air's an airline that flies to a desert.'

'Quick, man!' yelled Links. 'Say yes! We *do* want to know more.'

'Yes,' shouted the others. 'Say yes!'

Wills picked up the stick between his teeth. Spelling wasn't easy and hitting the right keys with a stick was even harder. Slowly, he prodded Y, then E, then S. Nothing happened. Then he remembered what he had to do next. He gripped the stick firmly and poked 'ENTER'. The aeroplane on the screen zoomed backwards and forwards, then landed in front of a blazing sun.

'So far so good . . .' said Wills.

He nearly jumped out of his fleece when a strange voice suddenly came from the laptop.

'Your battery is low,' it said.

Wills dropped the stick and stepped back, alarmed.

'Your battery is low,' the voice said again. 'It must be charged at once.'

'Anything you say,' grunted Oxo and he lowered his head.

'Charge your battery at once,' ordered the voice.

And before Wills could stop him, Oxo took a little run and smashed his head into the laptop. It crashed to the barn floor, where it lay with a shattered screen and a hole in the keyboard. The sheep stared at the wreckage.

'Ohmygrass . . .' said Jaycey. 'You've killed it.'

'The important thing is,' said Sal, 'that we said yes. We said yes and it understood. You all saw the aeroplane and the hot sun.' She beamed around at them. 'We're on our way to America!'

Wills was doubtful, but then they heard a screech of tyres and a loud engine.

'It's the aeroplane!' cried Sal. 'Come for us so soon?'

'Ooh, I'm not ready,' bleated Jaycey. 'I can't go to America in this state . . .'

She started rubbing her hooves on an obliging hen to make them shine.

'It can't be an aeroplane,' said Wills. 'We'll need a truck or something to take us to an airport first.'

They peered out into the farmyard. Wills was right. There was no aeroplane. Only tyre tracks in the mud and a pair of shiny shoes.

'A truck, you say, dear?' asked Sal. 'Well, I'm sure Desert Air will send one. Let's go outside and enjoy some good Eppingham grass while we're waiting.'

'I'll eat to that,' said Oxo and he led the way.

Still in the barn, Wills turned and looked back at the laptop, wondering if Ida would be very upset when she saw what had happened. And he still wasn't sure how he could have arranged a trip to America so easily when it took Ida hours, and sometimes lots of rude words, to make the laptop buy a bag of corn. But there was nothing else he could do, so he went outside to graze and hoped for the best.

Links was already composing his first Red Tongue rap.

'We's usually quiet and don't make no fuss,
But you evil guys shouldn't mess with us.
The Lambad dude thought he'd got us beat,
But he's history now and life is sweet.
We've been called again and we's heading West,
So, monster dude, you'll be messin' with the best.
"Red Tongue," you said. "Remember the name."
Well we's the Warrior Sheep, man.
You'd better do the same.'

The other sheep all raised their heads in a bleating chorus.

'Yeah, we's the Warrior Sheep, man. You'd better do the same.'

While they were singing, Tod came out of the farmhouse with a bucket of cabbage leaves. He was surprised to see the sheep gathered noisily near the paddock gate, as if they were waiting for something.

23

He grinned to himself: if only they knew they were on their way to America! He gave them their cabbage treat, then went into the barn to feed the hens and check out Rhubarb on Gran's laptop.

Wills stopped singing and watched Tod go into the barn. A few minutes later the boy came out again with the broken laptop in his arms. But he didn't look crossly at the sheep. He even waved as he went back into the farmhouse. Wills was relieved.

'The sheep are fine, Gran,' Tod called as he slipped his boots off. 'But I can't check out Rhubarb. Look what the hens have done to your laptop!'

4
The Boombergs

While the Rare Breed Warriors chomped in the paddock and Tod and Ida scurried around packing, an air stewardess was carrying bales of straw into a small private jet.

The jet was parked on a disused airfield, and its cabin had been divided into two sections. In the front section, there was a single row of seats. At the back, behind a partition, there were no seats at all; only a pen for animals. A man dressed in a pilot's uniform was helping spread the straw.

'Smithy was in a funny mood,' said the stewardess, whose name was Jo. 'He just took his money and ran. He looked very hot.'

'Perhaps he's eaten something that doesn't agree with him,' said Don, the pilot. 'Is this the first time we've done sheep? I only remember cats, dogs and horses.'

Jo nodded.

'Why does the customer want them in such a hurry?' asked Don.

'I didn't ask. I never do. I suppose she's just getting round the quarantine rules, like they all are.' Jo grinned. 'What do we care, Don? She's paying us a fortune.'

Animals were being discussed elsewhere too. Not in a field, but in a very secret place, way off the beaten track in the Arizona desert. Arizona, America.

In a room lit only by the glow from banks and banks of computers, a number of men and women were glaring fiercely at each other across a long table. Their angry faces looked weirdly grey in the light from the computer monitors. Most of them wore grubby white cotton coats over jeans and T-shirts.

At the head of the table, a hunched, frowning man, Professor Stanley Boomberg, was scribbling numbers on a sheet of paper and constantly referring to a mini computer attached to his wrist. He had a row of pencils slotted into the breast pocket of his clean white coat and two more stuck out of his ears. He was trying to ignore his noisy companions.

'Dogs!' a man on one side of the table shouted. 'It's got to be dogs.'

'Too stupid,' murmured Professor Boomberg.

Nobody heard. The scientists rarely bothered to listen to the Professor, even though he was their boss. Not unless his wife, prickly by name and prickly by nature, was around.

'We can't sacrifice dogs,' yelled a woman. 'They're so loyal.'

'That's right,' said another man. 'Cats. We must use cats.'

'You only say that because you don't like them,' replied a woman opposite.

'That's not the point,' shouted the man. 'We should use them because they're smart. Selfish but smart.'

'Nothing wrong with being selfish,' murmured Professor Boomberg, without looking up.

'Look, we should have made a decision weeks ago,' shouted the first man. He banged his fist on the table. 'Dogs!'

'Cats!' cried all the dog lovers, scraping their chairs back and standing up.

'Dogs!'

'Cats!'

The shouting went on and on.

'Pigs!' cried someone, trying to break the deadlock.

'Much *too* intelligent,' murmured the Professor, scrolling through the complicated figures on his wrist-top computer.

Except for the Professor, they were all on their feet now, yelling at each other, when the door suddenly burst open and the Professor's wife, Holly Boomberg, strode into the room. She wore a smart black suit, carried a briefcase and her red high-heeled shoes clacked in a business-like way on the tiled floor. Mrs Boomberg was an organiser, not a scientist, and she was very pleased with what she'd just organised.

'It's all fixed, darling,' she announced, patting the Professor's bony shoulder.

His pencil skidded, making a thick grey line across his calculations. He sighed. Holly took the other pencils from his ears.

'I've just had a call from the pilot, dear. The sheep are on their way.'

'Sheep?' Everyone stared at Mrs Boomberg and sat down, shocked.

'We can't use *sheep*,' squeaked one of the women. 'They're even more stupid than dogs.'

'Not these ones,' said Mrs Boomberg crisply. 'These ones are perfect for the job. You have my word for it.' She looked round the table. 'Don't you people have other computer screens to stare at?'

One grubby white coat eventually stood up again, then the others followed. Rather like sheep, thought Holly to herself as they filed out.

As soon as they'd gone, she slammed the door behind them, turned back to her husband and gave his bony shoulder an enthusiastic whack. He winced. Because he often forgot to eat, Stanley was thin and pale and not very strong. His wife, who took care of her health as efficiently as she took care of everything else, was super fit.

'These are exceptionally bright sheep, Stanley,' she bubbled. 'I remember seeing them on TV in England, last time I visited Mother. They saved a boy's life by stopping a train.'

'No kidding?' said the Professor, trying to sound interested. He *was* interested, of course. He needed animals for B-Day, and these sheep sounded perfect,

29

but he wished Holly would just go and get them without bothering him.

'Absolutely true, darling,' said Holly. 'They're amazing animals. We've got five coming, so you can choose the two you want and dump the rest.'

'Great, great . . .'

'I'm afraid their owners are coming too, which is annoying. But I have a plan for them.'

'I'm sure you do, honey,' said Stanley, flinching to avoid another whack or, worse, a kiss. 'Uh . . . how come we're getting them so quickly? Aren't there laws about bringing animals into the States?'

'Oh yes,' said Holly breezily. 'You can't. Not without permission. And they're supposed to go into quarantine for ages to make sure they're not carrying any nasty germs or worms or whatever.' She smiled reassuringly. 'But we haven't got time for all that, so I found a little firm in England who transport things privately, no questions asked.'

Stanley gulped. 'That must be costing you a lot of bucks, honey.'

Holly shrugged. 'It's only money,' she said. Then she smiled. 'With my money and your brains, we're a force to be reckoned with, Stanley Boomberg.'

Stanley nodded. His eyes suddenly gleamed and his thin lips stretched into a smile. 'And soon the world will know it.'

'Indeed it will,' said Holly. 'We shall be rich *and* famous.' Then she turned and her red high-heels clacked briskly towards the door. 'Now, they'll be arriving at dawn,' she said, 'and we must both be there to meet them.'

Stanley opened his mouth to protest. He didn't want to meet the owners. He didn't like people. And there were so many calculations still to do before B-Day. But it was too late. His wife had gone, pulling the door firmly shut behind her.

Back across the Atlantic, a small lorry pulled up outside Eppingham Farm. Oxo lowered his head, ready to batter the paddock gate open to get to it, but before he could charge, Tod hurried out of the farmhouse and unhooked the catch. Oxo was surprised and a bit disappointed.

Tod watched the sheep trot through the gateway and up the plank into the back of the lorry, then he shut the tailboard and the lorry drove away. Minutes later, a car drew up for Gran and himself. They squeezed in with their luggage.

'The sheep were so docile,' Tod said, as they settled down for the journey to the airport. 'It was like they were *expecting* to go for a ride.'

'You're letting your imagination run away with you,' said Gran. Then she pinched his arm. 'Are we really off to a convention in America?'

'We're Rhubarb's guests,' giggled Tod. 'Maybe they'll call me custard.'

'And what about me?' asked Gran.

'You can be crumble.'

Tod laughed and ducked to avoid Gran's pretend slap.

'Cheeky boy,' she said.

After an hour or so, the car turned off the main road into some lanes, then into a huge field with a grass runway at the far end. A small jet aeroplane was waiting for them.

'Doesn't look much like Heathrow,' said Tod, peering out of the car window.

The lorry had stopped close to the plane and the

sheep were already trotting up the ramp into the rear section of the cabin. Tod and Gran hurried across and waved until the door closed behind the sheep, then they turned to the front end where the stewardess was waiting for them. She didn't even glance at Gran's tickets as she ushered them up the steps.

'Are we the only passengers?' asked Tod, staring at the single row of seats.

'Yes,' smiled the hostess. 'This is a very exclusive airline. My name's Jo and you're travelling first class with us today. Now, if you'll fasten your seatbelts, we're ready for take-off.'

On the other side of the partition, the Warriors didn't have seatbelts but they did have plenty of straw and a big trough of fodder.

'How kind of Tod and Ida to see us off,' said Sal.

'Yeah,' agreed Oxo. 'But how did they know we're going West to butt Red Tongue's butt?' He lowered his head and got stuck into a mouthful of greens from the trough. 'Have I missed something?'

Wills had been worrying about the same thing. 'Maybe they saw a message on the laptop,' he said. 'A note from Desert Air.'

'No way,' said Jaycey, pleased to have thought of something Wills hadn't. 'Oxo killed the laptop, remember?'

'Maybe Tod mended it,' persisted Wills.

He couldn't think how else Tod and Ida could have found out.

Just then, the plane, which had been moving slowly, accelerated down the runway.

'Ohmygrass . . .' wailed Jaycey, forgetting her little moment of triumph.

Engines roared and lights flashed past the windows as the plane raced along. Then its wheels left the ground and it climbed sharply, sending the sheep rolling in the straw.

'Wicked!' shouted Links.

'Bye bye, Tod and Ida,' shouted Wills.

'Keep growing the cabbages,' called Oxo.

'Bye bye, rain,' squealed Jaycey.

Sal was all of a flutter.

'Fly us to the West!' she cried. 'Where the hottest winds blow!'

A few inches away in the passenger seats, Tod and Ida were just as excited. When the plane had finished climbing, Jo gave them a delicious supper and showed a funny film. Then, a little later, they stretched out on the seats and she covered them with soft, warm blankets.

'I'm too excited to sleep,' whispered Tod as Jo dimmed the cabin lights.

'Me too,' whispered Gran.

A few minutes later they were both snoring gently. They were still sleeping when the plane touched down to refuel . . . and when it took off again.

Hours later, Jo gently shook her passengers awake.

'Please fasten your seatbelts, ready for landing,' she said. 'It's five o'clock in the morning local time and the temperature outside is twenty-five degrees.'

The Warriors had also slept soundly, lulled by the engine noise and their full stomachs, but they were awake now. They got to their feet, refreshed and eager.

'I can see lights,' said Wills, peeping through the window. 'We're coming in to land.'

The wheels bumped down and the plane raced along the runway before jerking to a halt.

'We're in America!' breathed Wills.

'Red Tongue, your day of reckoning has arrived,' called Sal.

'We're the Warrior Sheep, Remember the name!' chorused the others.

Watching from the edge of the car park, Holly Boomberg gripped her husband's hand in excitement. He tried to ignore the pain.

'You did bring the sensors, honey?' he asked.

Holly patted her jacket pocket. 'Of course,' she said. 'All ready, darling.'

5

The Chosen Ones

'It's another tiny airport,' said Tod, as he and Gran walked away from the plane towards a chain-link fence at the edge of the field.

'Still, at least we won't have to wait for our luggage,' said Gran.

The pilot was striding in front of them, carrying their bags. Tod and Gran paused and glanced back. Jo was shooing their sheep into a shed in the opposite corner of the field. She'd told them that animals always had to go that way.

'They look fine,' said Tod.

The pilot marched through a gate in the fence, heading for the car park, and Tod and Gran had to run to keep up with him. None of the sheep noticed Tod and Ida. They were too busy trying to keep up with Jo.

'Ohmygrass . . .' said Jaycey, as they trotted into the shed. 'It's sooo hot!'

'And the sun's not even up yet,' observed Wills, glancing up at the dawn sky.

'Excellent,' said Sal. 'This *must* be the right West. We want the West where the sun scorches fleeces.'

'And the hottest winds blow,' grunted Links, moving away from Oxo, who'd rather overdone the greens on the plane and was having a gassy time digesting them.

As Tod and Gran arrived in the car park, Holly Boomberg squeezed her husband's hand again.

'Right, darling,' she said. 'These must be the owners. Now, do you remember what you have to do?'

'Drive them to Back of Beyond Ranch,' said Stanley reluctantly.

'And?'

Stanley pulled a face. 'Be charming.'

'You can if you try,' said Holly firmly. Then her voice became brisk again. 'The sheep transporter I ordered should be here any minute. As soon as it comes, I'll follow you to the ranch and you can choose the two you want.'

The pilot had reached the Boombergs' car. It was the only one in the car park. He dumped Tod's and Ida's bags beside it and then hurried back to the plane.

'Remember,' whispered Holly into Stanley's ear. 'You're from the Society for Rare, Humble, Unwanted, Beautiful And Rare Breeds.'

Panic spread across the Professor's face. 'I'm what? Tell me again.'

'You're Rhubarb.'

She gave him a little shove and strode away towards the shed, flashing a breezy smile at Tod and Ida as she went.

'I'm rhubarb, rhubarb, rhubarb . . .' muttered the Professor, walking slowly towards his car, his shoulders hunched, his head down.

He was still muttering when he came face to face with his supposed guests.

'Good morning,' the old lady said politely. 'I'm Ida White and this is my great-grandson Tod.'

'I'm Rhubarb,' Professor Boomberg announced. There was a pause. He didn't know what else to say, so he opened the car door and gestured for them to get in.

It was a very long, low car, black with black windows. Stanley turned up the air conditioning, handed Tod the remote for the TV and showed him how to get cold drinks from the mini fridge.

'Uh, let's go,' he said, sliding into the driver's seat.

'What about our sheep?' asked Gran.

'They'll be right behind,' said Stanley, even managing a smile. 'My wife will be bringing them.'

'Is this your wife now?' asked Gran, looking through the tinted windows at the woman in red high-heels marching across the car park towards them. 'She looks rather cross.'

Holly was cross.

'I'm so sorry about this delay,' she gushed, peering in at the open window. 'Do make yourselves at home for a few moments while we sort out the, er, formalities.' She turned to face her husband and spoke out of the corner of her mouth. 'Come with me, Stanley.'

Stanley didn't argue. He slid out of the car and followed her to the shed.

'You can't trust anyone to do anything right,' said Holly as she marched. 'I ordered a lorry and look what they've sent!'

Parked behind the shed was a small, open-topped buggy, the sort of thing used by golfers.

'And the idiots are blaming *me*. They thought I said buggy when I clearly said lorry!' She turned to face Stanley. 'Well, we can't get five sheep in this thing. You're going to have to choose here and now.'

Stanley started to flap his hands and tut. He hated being rushed.

'OK,' he said, 'I'll get the brain scanner from the car.'

'There's no time for that,' said Holly. 'This *is* illegal. And the pilot wants us to go. Now!' She pushed open the shed door and hurried inside. Five pairs of eyes turned towards her. 'Which two do you think?'

Stanley followed her in and shut the door peevishly. 'I don't know by just looking at them, do I?'

'I did tell you they're all bright,' his wife reminded him.

'I know, but I'm a scientist. I have to conduct some sort of intelligence test.' Stanley looked irritably round the shed. 'Ah.'

He'd seen a pile of buckets by the wall next to a bin of animal feed. He hurried across, took three buckets and stood them in a row. Then, while the sheep watched, he took a handful of feed from the bin. With a flourish, he dropped one of the round, grape-sized nuts of food into the first bucket. Then he dropped two nuts into the second. The third he left empty.

'Pass me that newspaper, honey,' he instructed.

Holly glanced at her watch but fetched the old newspaper her husband was pointing at and handed it to him. He placed a folded page over the top of each bucket.

'The smartest animals,' he said to Holly, 'will remember which bucket has the most food and head straight for it.' He folded his arms and stared at the sheep.

They stared right back.

'What's all that about?' asked Oxo.

The sheep had eaten well on the plane and not even he fancied a snack yet.

'No idea,' said Wills.

Jaycey suddenly noticed that the empty bucket was shinier than the other two. She trotted across to it.

'Ohmygrass . . .' she moaned, peering at her

reflection in its side. 'Just look what this heat is doing to my fleece already . . .'

Holly was standing beside her husband with the clipboard she always carried in her briefcase.

'Cross that one off,' said the Professor. 'It went straight for the empty bucket.'

Wills followed Jaycey. With his teeth, he gripped the newspaper from the top of the empty bucket and dropped it on to the floor.

'If I can find a map,' he said, 'I might be able to tell exactly where we are.'

'Just as stupid as the first one,' declared the Professor. 'Cross it off.'

'Are you sure, darling?' Holly was watching Wills. 'It actually looks quite bright to me.'

The Professor raised his eyebrows. 'Honey, do I tell you how to go about organising things?'

'Sorry, darling.'

Holly bit her lip. Stanley only ever contradicted her when they were talking about something scientific. And she always let him. He was, after all, the cleverest scientist in the world. Or so she believed.

They watched the sheep silently for a few moments,

43

then Holly glanced at her watch again and began tapping her fingers anxiously on her clipboard. Links got to his feet and walked away.

'She got no rhythm, man,' he muttered. 'That is painful on the ears.'

'Cross it off?' asked Holly.

'Cross it off,' said Stanley.

'So we take the remaining two?'

'Just let me make quite sure.'

The Professor dredged a handful of feed nuts from the bin, held them high in the air, then dropped the lot noisily into the empty bucket. Then he opened up another sheet of newspaper and with a dramatic flourish laid it across the top.

Something scarily familiar caught Oxo's eye. He stiffened.

'Do you see what I saw?' he asked.

Only he and Sal had been watching.

'A red tongue,' she breathed. 'On the bucket.'

'Just like the one on the laptop thingy?' asked Oxo.

'Exactly like it,' said Sal. 'Is it a pop-up?'

'No,' growled Oxo. 'It's a challenge.'

He lowered his head and charged. Sal did the

same. The shiny bucket with its handful of nuts went spinning across the shed. The sheet of newspaper covering it was shredded under two sets of hooves as they trampled the printed image of Red Tongue.

The Boombergs retreated hastily to the top of a stack of hay bales.

'Awesome,' murmured the Professor. 'They homed in like missiles.'

Holly took a coil of rope from her briefcase and tied it in a slip-knot. She stood up, ready to take aim. There was no escape.

6
The Staple Gun

'What's up?' asked Wills, as he, Jaycey and Links ran to join Oxo and Sal by the upturned bucket.

'Red Tongue!' panted Sal. She nosed the trampled newspaper.

'Ooh . . . have we killed him already?' gasped Jaycey.

'No, dear,' said Sal. 'This is only a pretend one. We were practising.'

Wills peered at a torn headline.

'This is just talking about him,' he told Jaycey. 'It says, Red Tongue is . . .'

'What?' asked Oxo. 'As good as dead?'

'No,' said Wills. 'It says, Red Tongue is on the road!' He looked up, pleased. 'That's good. All we have to do is find the road.'

'Easy,' said Oxo. 'Let's go.'

But as he turned to the door, his eyes suddenly bulged and a choking noise gurgled from his throat. Beside him, Sal was bulging and choking too. From on top of the hay bales, Holly Boomberg had thrown her rope and caught them both in the one noose.

'Hold them,' she instructed, handing the rope to Stanley. 'Pull as tight as you need. Just keep them still.'

'I *can't* hold them!' cried Stanley, digging his feet into the hay and clutching the rope to his chest. 'Honey, what are you doing?'

'Isn't it obvious, dear?' asked Holly, jumping down to the floor. She had taken a very large staple gun from her briefcase and was fitting something into it as she edged towards the struggling sheep. 'My plan was to do this at the ranch, but I might as well attach the sensors now, while they're nicely trapped.'

She lunged forward, grabbed Sal's ear and deftly stapled a silver stud into it.

'Excellent . . .' she said, fitting a gold stud into the staple gun.

Oxo choked and strained helplessly. Holly turned to him, pushed her sleeves up a little so as not to dirty the cuffs, then grabbed one of his ears. With a snap, the gold stud was fired from the staple gun into his flesh.

'Ohmygrass . . .' wailed Jaycey. 'That must be sooo sore!'

Holly smiled up at her husband as she slipped the staple gun back into her briefcase. 'Back on track, darling,' she said. 'You can go back to the car now and drive the ancient shepherdess and her boy out to the ranch. I'll take these two back to site in that stupid buggy thing. They'll just about fit.'

'What about the others, honey?' asked Stanley, slithering down from the hay bales, the rope still clutched to his chest.

Holly shrugged. 'They're no use to us now. They can stay here.'

'They'll die without water,' observed Stanley, though his glance at Jaycey, Wills and Links was unconcerned.

'That's what sheep are supposed to do, isn't it?' said Holly, barely listening. 'Die and get eaten.'

She opened the door a crack and peeped out. Don, the pilot, was pacing up and down close to the plane. He saw Holly and tapped his watch angrily.

'Do hurry, darling,' Holly said to Stanley. 'The pilot's going to explode if we don't get away from here soon.'

'OK, OK, I'm gone.' The Professor dropped the rope and hurried to the door. 'Stay in touch.'

He disappeared, leaving the door open. Sunlight poured in and the sheep made an instinctive bid for freedom. Holly stooped and swiftly grabbed up the rope trailing from Sal's and Oxo's necks. She hauled them back, the noose tightening around their throats, making them choke and cough again.

'*I'll* say when we leave,' she told them, stepping back further to gain a better hold.

Then a strange, undignified thing happened. Her feet slid from under her and continued to slide, no matter how hard she tried to stay upright. It was like running uphill backwards on roller skates. It didn't work. And after a few seconds, she was flat on her back. She clung on to the rope but her bottom was sliding now as well as her feet.

In the moment before she collided painfully with the wall and lost her grip on the rope, Holly was sure she glimpsed the skinny brown lamb standing beside the feed bin. The bin was lying on its side now, its load of feed nuts bouncing across the floor like a thousand organic marbles. Surely he couldn't have turned it over! What's more, she thought she saw the lamb clacking front hooves with the curly-haired ram. She certainly saw him scamper across to where Stanley's chosen sheep were trying to get through the door at the same time. The skinny brown lamb – the one her husband had dismissed as stupid – trod on the noose so that the captives could back their heads out of the circle of rope as it slackened.

Then they were all gone, and Holly was left with nothing but a large headache. She stumbled to her feet, kicking feed nuts in all directions, and rushed outside. The desert beyond the fence appeared entirely sheep-less. She heard a sound and span round. Don, the pilot, was walking quickly towards the plane. Jo had already shut the passenger door.

'My sheep have escaped!' cried Holly, running after the pilot. 'You've got to help me get them back!'

Don turned briefly and frowned at her.

'Sheep?' he said. 'What sheep?'

7
Chased Down

Tod and Gran were standing beside the car, gazing at the stark landscape beyond the chain-link fence, when Stanley returned.

'Uh . . . sorry to keep you waiting,' he said, picking hay from his jacket. 'It was the uh . . .'

'Formalities?' offered Gran.

'Sure.' Their host nodded. 'The formalities.'

'Are our sheep OK?' asked Tod.

'They're being loaded right now,' said Stanley.

Reassured, Tod and Gran clambered back into the luxury of the biggest car they had ever seen. The sun continued to rise behind them as their host drove from the car park and on to the straight, empty road. There were no houses, no trees, no people – just barren flatness. It was only broken by great slabs of mountain in the distance, rising in sheer cliffs that were blood-red in colour, turning to orange as the sky above hardened to bright blue.

'Beautiful, isn't it?' whispered Tod.

'Amazing,' agreed Gran. She squeezed his hand and giggled. 'A bit different from Eppingham.'

'I wonder where the conference centre is,' Tod said. 'Shall I ask?'

Gran nodded, but before Tod had a chance to speak, the car jolted to a halt and they were thrown forward by the abrupt stop.

'We've what?' they heard the Professor snap into his mobile phone.

They couldn't hear the other end of the conversation, but Stanley could. His wife's voice was loud and clear.

'We've lost the sheep,' she repeated, sharply. 'Act like nothing's wrong. Keep driving.'

Tod and Ida were thrown backwards as the car lurched on again.

'The idiot pilot wouldn't help me catch them,' Holly continued. 'Anyway, I haven't exactly lost them. I'm on their trail. Keep going until you hear from me again. And be charming to our guests. Distract them. Point out all the interesting things you pass.'

'We're in a desert,' said the Professor. 'There *aren't* any interesting things.'

'You're a scientist,' snapped his wife. 'Invent some.'

And she ended the call.

Holly Boomberg had indeed found a trail. A scuffle in the dirt behind the airfield shed had settled into a steady line of hoofprints that soon joined the desert road – the same road Stanley had taken only a few minutes earlier. The only road, in fact.

Stupid animals, she thought. Where did they think they were going? They'd be dead within a day. She had to save them – well, Stanley's chosen two. The rest could become vulture meat for all she cared.

Holly had got over the shock of the sheep's escape; convinced herself it had just been bad luck. No sheep could be *that* clever. She was feeling confident again. She leapt into the golf buggy and drove off in a dramatic swirl of dust.

Some way ahead in the shadeless desert, the Warriors had slowed from a headlong race to a brisk trot.

After a while, Sal said, 'We *are* going the right

way, aren't we, dear?'

She was sure Wills had once said something about using the sun to know where you were.

Wills' short legs had to move fast to keep up.

'Yes,' he gasped. 'The sun's behind us. It rises in the East, so we know we're heading West.'

'That's what I thought,' said Sal and she broke into a gallop again. 'Onward, brave Warriors!' she cried.

Wills tried to speak but his voice got lost in the thunder of hooves and heavy breathing.

Jaycey glanced at Sal and Oxo as she ran. It must have hurt when the Staple Gun Woman put the studs in their ears, but they did look very bling, glinting silver and gold in the sunlight. They were, she thought, wasted on Oxo and Sal.

Oxo had forgotten all about the gold stud in his ear. The complete absence of grub was a much greater concern. There was simply no grass. He'd tried a nibble of one of the grey stunted trees dotted about the place, but it was dry and bitter – a poor second even to an Eppingham fence post. The spiny cactus plants were greenish but, whichever way you came at them, they gave you a bloody nose. He was fed up with not being fed.

'What's the point of a place where there's no point stopping for breakfast?' he complained as he ran.

'What did you expect, man?' said Links. 'It's the desert, innit.'

Wills finally made his voice heard.

'I think we should slow down!' he called to Sal, who was still in the lead but now panting heavily.

She skidded to a halt, then, after a moment, walked on slowly, her sides heaving.

'West is west,' she puffed, 'and Red Tongue's about to meet the best . . .'

'Right,' said Wills. 'But we've set off too fast.'

Behind him, he heard Links beginning a new rap, his voice croaky but determined.

'We ain't never been so hot before,
But we gotta show Red Tongue the door,
We got a job and it's gotta be done,
So it's no use complainin' 'bout the sun.
We know we can take it, cos we is tough,
The Warrior Sheep ain't never had enough . . .

The Warrior Sheep ain't never had enough . . .'

He sang quietly at first, nodding his head and flicking his damp curls from his eyes as he walked. The others listened and then joined in, gradually getting louder and stronger as they stopped puffing. Their plod became a march, their necks straightened and their spirits rose.

'The Warrior Sheep ain't never had enough . . .'

A little way behind them but catching up fast, Holly Boomberg stopped to take a drink from the bottle of water in the golf buggy. She was no longer angry at the size of the vehicle. Or its lack of air conditioning. It went surprisingly fast and she only had to glance out of the open sides as she drove to follow the trail. She could still see the sheep's hoofprints. She ran a comb through her hair, slicked on a smear of lipgloss and drove confidently on. It could only be a matter of minutes now.

The Warriors sang until they were too hot to sing any more, and then they marched in silence. They reached a long line of billboards at the side of the road.

'I'm sooo thirsty . . .' whimpered Jaycey as they passed the boards.

'Yeah, and my stomach thinks my mouth's been tied shut,' said Oxo.

Wills stopped and craned his neck to look up at the boards. His heart skipped a beat.

'Hey, wait a minute,' he called. 'Look at this!'

There, way above their heads, were tongues. A whole line of Red Tongues. And under the pictures were words. Wills squinted into the glaring light.

RED TONGUE'S GONNA SLAUGHTER THE RAMS.

WHERE?

FORT WILMOT, LAS VEGAS

THEN

ARIES END.

BE THERE!

Wills read the words to himself, then aloud.

'Ohmygrass . . .' whispered Jaycey. 'Is that a message for us? Like the pop-up?'

'I think it must be,' said Wills, still squinting up

into the sun. His head suddenly started to spin and then his legs buckled under him.

'Sorry, guys . . .' he said, feeling dizzy. 'I seem to be sitting down . . .'

'It's the sun, innit,' said Links, giving him a little nudge. 'Get in the shade.'

Wills wobbled to his hooves and they all stepped from the road, tottered round behind the billboards and flopped down. It was a relief to be out of the direct sunshine.

'We gotta rest here a few minutes, innit,' panted Links.

'Yes. We must pace ourselves if we're to be fit for battle,' gasped Sal. 'I recall saying that earlier.'

Gradually, their breathing steadied and one by one they closed their eyes.

Seconds later, Holly Boomberg's buggy appeared. She didn't even glance at the billboards as she whizzed past. She was staring intently at the road, which had briefly become too hard and stony to show hoofprints, and was anxious to pick up the trail again. Her mobile phone rang. She heard Stanley's stiff voice.

'Did you find the sheep yet?'

'Almost, dear. Are you being charming to our guests?'

'Almost. They're getting twitchy. Do you realise how many prickly pears we have in Arizona?'

'All will be well, darling,' Holly assured him. 'Just get them to the ranch.'

She made a little kissing noise and switched off before he could tell her how busy he was and how many calculations he had to do before B-Day. Let the white-coated scientists he employed do a few, she thought. That was, after all, what she was paying them for.

Stanley glared in the rear-view mirror at his passengers. He longed to be rid of them but his wife was right: keep them happy.

'Oh, look!' he said. 'Over on your right. A very fine example of . . . uh, another prickly pear.'

Tod and Gran had already seen hundreds of prickly pears. They looked at each other then turned and peered through the rear window yet again. There was still no sign of the truck carrying their sheep as they'd been promised.

'As soon as we stop,' Tod whispered, 'I'm going to find a phone and call the police.'

'Agreed,' said Gran. 'There's something fishy going on here.'

The Warriors had dozed in the shade for only a few minutes, but it was enough to revive them. With Oxo in the lead, they stepped out from behind the billboards, back on to the stony road.

'Onward?' asked Oxo, already feeling the sun beating down on him again.

'Onward!' the others cried, half closing their eyes against the glare.

They marched on, the air so hot now it seemed to burn in their noses as they breathed. Their throats felt parched and even Links couldn't manage to sing.

After a while, they paused to catch their breath by a signpost stuck crookedly into the ground.

'What does it say, dear?' panted Sal.

'Fort Wilmot via Dead Man's Creek . . .' gasped Wills. 'Fort Wilmot! Red Tongue's there!'

'Dead Man's Creek,' grunted Oxo. 'Sounds inviting.'

'What if it's Dead *Lamb's* Creek too?' whimpered Jaycey.

'It's taking us towards Red Tongue,' said Sal. 'That's all that matters.'

They marched on.

'Anyway, what's a creek?' Oxo asked suddenly.

Wills had been trying to remember the same thing. He thought a creek was a sort of river but he didn't want to raise anyone's hopes so he didn't answer the question. Instead he said, 'Should we rest again for a moment?'

Sal's sides were heaving more than ever and she was beginning to stagger. She slumped to the ground but while the others gathered anxiously around her, Links stepped aside and raised his head. Listening.

'Uh, maybe sitting's not the best thing right now . . .' he said.

The others lifted their heads and heard what Links had heard: a noise in the distance behind them. A growl that rapidly became a roar. Staring in its direction, they saw a plume of dust.

'Ohmygrass . . .' squeaked Jaycey. 'Is it . . . is it . . . Red Tongue?'

'We's in no state to find out, man,' said Links. 'When in doubt . . . run!'

They prodded and heaved Sal to her feet and, forgetting their thirst and fatigue, ran for their lives. They galloped away along the road, their hearts pounding with fear. But the plume of dust behind them drew closer, and the roar grew louder, accompanied now by strange braying blasts.

Wills veered off the road and the other Warriors followed, but it was no use. The roar followed, getting closer and louder. The ground was rough here and strewn with boulders and prickly cacti, which they stumbled over and into. They all began to slow, their flanks heaving, their tongues swelling in their mouths. Then, one by one, they dropped to their knees and rolled on their sides, beyond panic, utterly exhausted. Tongues lolling as they gulped down breaths of stifling desert air, they awaited their fate.

8
On the Road

The braying roar was on top of them now, and Wills, who had closed his eyes, opened them again. He'd suddenly become aware of music as well as the roar. The kind of loud rock music that Ida sometimes played to the hens back in Eppingham. Wills blinked. The roar came from an engine. The braying was a vehicle horn. Looming above the Warriors, momentarily shutting out the blinding sun, was not a triumphant Red Tongue, but a large white convertible car with its roof folded back. Two teenage boys were craning over the windscreen.

'Aries, Aries . . .' they chanted. 'Rams, Ewes and Lambs!'

'Hey, Cameron,' said one of the boys as he switched off the music. 'That wasn't so cool after all.' He jumped out of the car. 'Look at them, they're pooped.' He knelt beside Sal. 'We shouldn't have chased them like that.'

'They'll get over it,' said his brother. 'Come on, Phoenix, let's go.'

But Phoenix glanced up, frowning. 'They're not even desert sheep. Look – they're kind of fluffy and fat.'

'I am sooo *not* fat,' croaked Jaycey, raising her head slightly before flopping down again.

'I wonder where they came from?' continued Phoenix.

'Does it matter? They're a bunch of sheep. Let's go.' Cameron revved the engine impatiently.

'No,' said Phoenix. 'We can't just leave them in this state.'

'So what d'you want to do, take them with us?'

'Cool idea,' said Phoenix, straightening up. 'Give me a hand.'

'Are you crazy? What's Mom gonna say, filling her pride and joy with livestock?'

'Can't do it any more damage than your driving. Come on, grab a leg.'

Cameron reluctantly did as he was asked, and between them the brothers heaved Sal off the ground and on to the back seat. When she regained consciousness a few seconds later, she found herself forehead to curly forehead with Links, who'd been swung in beside her.

'What's happening, man?' he asked weakly.

'I think we've had an out-of-body experience, dear . . .' replied Sal, before her voice and mind drifted away again.

'Oh,' said Links. 'I thought we was just thirsty.'

Then Jaycey was being lowered in between them. 'I am sooo not fat . . .' she continued to murmur. 'Sooo not fat . . .'

The car dipped and swayed as Oxo, having staggered to his feet, clambered on board with a helping shoulder from Phoenix, and wedged himself next to Links on the back seat.

'One to go,' said Phoenix, scooping up Wills.

'Well you'll just have to have him on your lap, bro,' replied Cameron. '*I'm* still driving.' And he got in quickly behind the wheel.

Wills didn't mind sitting on a lap, and he was feeling better now that his heart had stopped hammering. His tongue still felt like a lump of wood in his parched mouth but he lifted his head and gazed through the windscreen. The air that ruffled his fleece as the car suddenly shot backwards and swung round on to the road again was still hot but quite refreshing. He sat up straight to catch more of it. Behind him, the other Warriors were also struggling upright to catch the welcome breeze.

'Do we have any water left?' asked Phoenix.

'Only juice,' said Cameron.

Phoenix pulled a handful of plastic bottles from the cool box by his feet and held one in front of Wills. It had a sucker top and, after a few false starts, Wills managed to suck up some liquid. Cameron stopped the car and both boys leaned around to offer bottles to the other sheep. They sucked desperately, finally got the hang of it and drank, relieving their parched tongues and throats.

Jaycey dropped her empty bottle and stared, mesmerised, at Cameron's sunglasses. How cool were they? Cooler than those silly old ear studs Oxo and Sal were wearing. She fluttered her eyelids and tossed her pretty head.

Cameron grinned, faced the front again and aimed the car West. 'Aries, Aries, Rams, Ewes and

Lambs!' he sang. 'Tell you what, Phee, they make the greatest mascots.'

In the back seat, Sal, who didn't understand much humanspeak, stiffened.

'Uh, Wills dear,' she asked anxiously, leaning forward, 'what exactly are mascots?'

Wills couldn't remember. But he didn't think they were cut-up and cookable, so he relaxed, letting his ears flap in the wind, and his tongue lick the last of the juice from his no-longer-parched lips.

Cameron thought roads were boring and constantly veered off to take the car jolting away across the stony desert, dodging boulders and cacti with last-second spins of the steering wheel. The Warriors, even Sal, loved every minute of the ride, and when Cameron leaned round and stuck his shades on Jaycey's head, she thought she'd gone to Sheep Heaven.

'Cool wheels, innit,' yelled Links.

'Excellent,' called back Wills.

The car sped on with the humans chanting and the sheep bleating and the sun burning in the blue sky above. They saw no other traffic until Cameron turned the car towards the road for the last time.

'Wave, guys,' he yelled, turning the music up even louder. 'Some dude's coming our way.'

Holly Boomberg couldn't remember where she'd last seen hoofprints. Before the billboards, she thought, but she'd gone way past them before she'd realised and turned back. Now she was angry with herself and driving fast, peering at the dusty road.

Suddenly, a white car bounced from the desert and came racing towards her, veering dangerously from side to side. She slowed down and the white car shot past, music blaring, the occupants singing. Singing and *bleating*! Holly stamped on the brakes, pulled over and twisted around in her seat. She hadn't imagined it. The sheep, *her* sheep, were sitting on the back seat. And one of them was wearing sunglasses. She swallowed hard, took a deep breath, turned the buggy around and gave chase.

None of the Warriors recognised the driver of the golf buggy, nor did they see it turn in the road and start following. Cameron saw and punched the air.

'Yeehaa!' he yelled. 'The dude wants a race!'

He swung the car off the road again and surged over the desert.

'Holy sheep!' exclaimed Phoenix, hanging on to the edge of his seat. 'What are you doing now?'

'Get ready to rock and roll,' yelled Cameron. 'Dead Man's Creek coming up!'

The creek ran parallel with the road and Wills had been right. It was a sort of river; only it was completely dried up. It hadn't carried a drop of water for months.

Holly drove as fast as she could along the road but her buggy couldn't keep pace. She could only watch as the white car careered up and down the steep banks of the dried-up creek. It was like looking down on a never-ending rollercoaster but soon the white car was out of sight and she was following a cloud of dust.

'Idiot!' she shouted, as if the driver could hear her. 'Kill yourselves if you want, but not Stanley's sheep!'

Inside the white car, Phoenix grabbed Wills tight to stop the lamb being catapulted out.

'You're crazy,' he yelled at his brother. 'You'll turn us over!'

Cameron just laughed, spun the wheel and shot

the car from the bottom of the creek to the top of its steep bank.

'Yeehaa!' he cried as he turned at the top.

'Stop!' yelled Phoenix.

But Cameron couldn't. His Mom's pride and joy had had enough. The brakes and the steering gave up at the same moment. The car plunged down, out of control.

'Ohmygrass . . . ohmyshades . . .' wailed Jaycey as the sunglasses sailed through the air in front of her.

The car bounced down the slope, turned over and over and landed right way up on the bottom of the creek.

There was a long moment's silence.

'Mom's gonna be so mad at me . . .' was all Cameron could say when he'd stopped shaking.

'I guess she'd sooner write off a car than two stupid sons,' replied Phoenix.

He let go of Wills and the lamb leapt out. Then Phoenix twisted around to look at the back seat.

'It's a good job the rest were wedged in so tight.'

Links was squeezing himself free. He clambered out over the side. Oxo followed, then Sal and Jaycey.

'Well that was, er, very nice,' said Sal, shaking herself. 'But it's time to press on, I think.'

'Onwards and . . . upwards?' asked Oxo, looking up at the steep sides of the creek. He started looking for a way to climb out.

The others did the same, but after only a few steps, Sal stopped. She twitched her ear. The silver stud in it was buzzing. The others paused and looked enquiringly at her.

'Most uncomfortable . . .' she said. 'Like having a fly inside my head . . .'

They could all hear the buzzing now. Cameron and Phoenix, still strapped into the car, heard it too. Suddenly, it changed to a high-pitched beeping.

But no one was looking at Sal any more. They were all, sheep and humans, staring straight past her at the wall of water rushing towards them.

9
Up the Creek

It was a flash flood, and it was on them in a flash. There had been a heavy storm in the distant mountains two days ago and the rain water had finally reached the dried-up creek. It was in a hurry and inescapable. It had swept up all manner of brushwood and dead cacti on its headlong journey and now it swept up the sheep and the car as well. This might have been fun, like white-water rafting, except there was no raft. There was only the rushing, swirling muddy torrent; and the likelihood of being dragged under by the current and drowned, or smashed to bits on the rocks. Or both.

Eventually, the white car stopped, upside down, jammed between the side of the creek and a huge rock. The Warriors were swirled against it and the torrent rushed on past them. There was no sign of

Cameron or Phoenix.

'They're trapped underneath!' cried Wills.

They could all hear the boys coughing and retching weakly as they tried to escape.

'We have to shift the car,' continued Wills, 'or they'll drown. Quick!'

'Man, I hate bein' sheep dipped,' said Links, but he breathed out and allowed himself to sink under the water.

All five Warriors were soon submerged, shoulder to shoulder in the roaring watery murk, their hooves scrabbling on slippery rocks. They put their heads against the side of the upturned car. They heaved once, they heaved twice. They heard a tinny grinding noise and heaved again. As they did so, their hooves stumbled forward and suddenly they were breathing fresh air again. The white car reared above them, then twisted and slid away through the narrow rocky gap that it had been blocking. It swirled on in the torrent.

Shocked and shivering, but free of the deadly metal prison, Phoenix and Cameron clambered up the side of the creek to safety.

73

The Warriors shook themselves and followed, picking their way across the boulders and loose rocks, then gathering in a huddle close to Cameron and Phoenix as the two brothers flopped to the ground.

'Way to go, sheep . . .' murmured Cameron, raising his hand in a feeble attempt at a high five. 'Aries, Aries . . . Rams, Ewes and Lambs . . .'

His eyes closed in utter exhaustion but, as they did, he was almost sure he saw the five sheep turn to each other, then raise and clack hooves.

It was getting dark now, and in different parts of the desert two sets of headlights were turned on.

The first were bright and beady, like the driver of the golf buggy who had flicked their switch. But even crouched in the headlight beam, Holly Boomberg had lost the trail again. How typical of Mother Nature, how very *inefficient* to have a flood right now!

Had the sheep got across? Were they all drowned? Had they got out of the creek on the same side they went in? In fact, they had, but the water had swept them a long, long way downstream. Holly couldn't see them. There were no tracks. There was nothing she could do. But doing nothing was not a Holly Boomberg mode. She got back into the buggy and turned downstream.

The other set of headlights were equally bright, but the mood in the back of Professor Boomberg's car was becoming very dark. His passengers had gone from polite, to politely suspicious, to extremely suspicious indeed.

'Look,' the old lady was saying, tapping him on the shoulder. 'Mr er . . . Rhubarb, can you please stop?'

'No,' Stanley said. 'Not yet.'

'At the next service station, then,' said the boy. 'One with a shop and a café.'

He didn't add, 'and one with telephones', but the Professor guessed that was what he meant. He clenched his teeth and drove on in silence.

'Look out for signposts,' whispered Gran. 'So we can tell the police where we are.'

They watched carefully as they sped along but there were no signs. They had never imagined a place could be so big and so empty. Some time later, Gran's bony knee nudged Tod's.

'His mobile's on the front seat,' she whispered.

'See if you can distract him while I pinch it and call the police.'

Tod gave her a silent OK then leaned forward and tapped Stanley on the shoulder.

'Excuse me. I *need* to stop,' he said. 'For a pee.'

The Professor slowed the car. 'Can't you wait?'

'No. I'm desperate.'

The Professor sighed and pulled up. 'Well go on then.'

Tod struggled with the door, pretending he couldn't open it.

'Help,' he pleaded, turning to the Professor, 'I'm *really* desperate.'

Stanley got out, paced to the rear door and pulled it open. Tod hopped out. The Professor glanced fretfully at his wrist computer.

'One hundred and seventy-eight thousand, seven hundred and ten seconds and counting . . .' he muttered to himself. 'So much still to do . . .' Then he saw the old lady tapping at his mobile phone. 'Hey!' he shouted, and dived into the car and snatched it from her. He turned angrily to Tod. 'Get back!' he ordered.

'What's going on?' Gran demanded as Tod ran back to be with her. She'd wriggled out of the car now. 'What's your *real* name? Where are our sheep? Where's the conference?'

'And where are you taking us?' added Tod.

'I really have no idea where your sheep are,' replied the Professor spitefully. 'There is no conference. And I'm taking you to Back of Beyond Ranch. So you're out of circulation till after B-Day.'

Tod and Gran simply gaped.

'At least I *was*.' Stanley got back behind the wheel and slammed his door. 'But I've had enough. You can walk.' He pointed into the darkening desert. 'It's that way!'

The car window slid up silently, and Tod and Gran could only watch, still gaping, as the sleek black car disappeared into the gathering dusk. The sound of its engine faded to nothing.

'D'you think he'll come back?' asked Tod.

'No,' said Gran definitely.

Tod stared around at the desert stretching away in all directions.

'Well,' he said. 'We'd better see if we can find

this Back of Beyond Ranch before it gets completely dark.'

'If it exists,' grunted Gran, and she delved in her bag for her trusty head torch.

Back of Beyond Ranch did exist. They reached it half an hour later. The faded name, just visible in the light of Gran's head torch, was scratched on a boulder at the side of the road. Beyond the boulder was a broken wooden fence that had long since given up surrounding a patch of baked earth covered in weedy weeds. In the middle of the baked earth was the ranch house. It had four stone walls but no roof. The windows had tattered curtains but no glass. A notice nailed to the front door read: GONE AWAY.

Tod pushed the door open and peeped in. A cockroach scuttled across the dirt floor. Then there was silence.

'At least we've got some shelter,' said Tod. 'I can't believe how cold it's getting now the sun's gone down.' He dragged in an old bench from outside and put it against the wall. 'Sit here, Gran. I'll see if I can find anything useful, like a phone.'

There was no phone, but in the yard outside he found a well, covered with a plank of wood, with a rusty tin bucket beside it.

'Drink this, Gran!' he said, returning and offering her an equally rusty mug full of water. 'You'll have to imagine the tea bag.'

Gran drank. 'Best I've ever tasted,' she said. 'And look what I've found for supper.'

Dumped in the corner of the room was a pile of plastic carrier bags full of tinned food: salmon, baked beans, soup.

'Looks like Rhubarb was telling the truth,' Gran said. 'He *was* planning to bring us here.'

'But why do they want us out of the way?' asked Tod, shaking his head. A cold feeling settled in the pit of his stomach as he thought about the flock. 'And what do you think they've done with our sheep, Gran?'

Gran tried to sound more confident than she felt.

'Your guess is as good as mine,' she said, 'but I'm sure they're fine.'

She shivered and pulled her thin cardigan around her shoulders. Tod immediately began gathering together all the dry sticks he could find.

'Have you got any matches?' he asked.

Gran poked about again in the bottomless pit that was her handbag, and dredged up a matchbox with one live match in it and thirty dead ones. Tod crossed his fingers, then uncrossed them again, struck the live match and held it to his little pile of kindling.

'Phew . . .' he said as it lit.

There was a newspaper in the bag of groceries. Tod handed it to Ida.

'Here, Gran, read this while I get some more wood.'

When he returned with an armful of broken fence posts and branches, Gran was engrossed in the newspaper.

'It's this week's,' she said. 'Not terribly useful, though. Nearly all about football. American football. Seems like there are two local teams slugging it out just now to be top of the league. One lot come from Aries End. Guess what their nickname is?'

Tod shrugged. 'Don't know.'

'They're called the Rams,' said Gran. 'How about that? The other lot come from a place called Fort Wilmot and they're the Prairie Dogs.' She grinned.

'And can you guess what *their* nickname is?'

Tod shook his head. 'Nope.'

'It's a funny one,' said Gran. 'They call themselves Red Tongue.'

10
Sandstorm

Everyone agreed: deserts were pants.

'First we get fried,' complained Jaycey, 'then we get flooded. Now we're getting frozen.' She counted on her hooves. 'That's three Fs all in one day, Sal, and only *one* of them was in the prophecy.' She nibbled fretfully at her once-beautiful fleece. 'Just look at my ends. I feel like a mouldy haystack. And you,' she said to Oxo, trying to shove him away as he settled closer beside her, 'smell like one.'

On her other flank, Links gave her a nudge.

'O' course we's gonna smell, if we's been in the river,
Cos we is fleeced up, man, but it helps us not to shiver.
Would you rather be an ovine?
Or a human with no wool?

Cos they is *really* cold, man, and not just
Sheeply cool.'

He nodded at Cameron and Phoenix. Their shirts
and jeans still damp, the boys had snuggled close to
the sheep as the sun had set and the temperature
plummeted. Finally, the sheep had formed a complete
ring around them, a warm woolly nest, and they were
both asleep.

'Like lambs,' cooed Sal. 'Strange they're not in the
prophecy.'

'There's a lot of things not in the prophecy, innit,'
said Links. 'Like Jaycey says. Starving's another one,
'cept it don't begin with F.'

'And Fort Wilmot and Las Vegas and Aries End . . .'
said Wills.

'The reason Aries End is not in the prophecy, dear,'
said Sal, 'is that Aries will *never* end.'

She snuggled closer to her human lambs and
fell asleep.

Professor Boomberg was warm enough in his car and
comfortable too, but there was no time to rest. He was

on his way back to base. He didn't phone his wife. She could catch the sheep on her own. He didn't doubt that she would and when she did, everything else needed to be ready. He glanced at his wrist computer.

'One hundred and seventy thousand seconds and counting . . .' he murmured.

He smiled his gleaming smile in the darkness. It was going to be tight but they would make it. B-Day *would* happen.

'I'll show them all,' he said aloud. 'They won't be calling me mad in a hundred and seventy thousand seconds' time!'

Holly Boomberg wasn't nearly so warm. The open-sided golf buggy wasn't designed for sleeping in, so she was glad of the lightweight sports blanket she always carried in her briefcase. She tucked it neatly around her shoulders and made herself as comfortable as possible. She'd parked the buggy beside the still-swollen creek. At first light she would search for tracks again. Failure was not an option. Everything depended on her. And the sheep.

Cameron and Phoenix were on their feet before sunrise.

'Mom's gonna be worried sick,' said Phoenix. 'Are you sure your phone's not working?'

'I've told you, man. Dead as a dodo,' replied Cameron, and he tossed his water-logged phone at his brother.

Phoenix prodded at it for a few seconds, then threw it on the ground. 'So what do we do now?'

'We walk,' said Cameron. He'd got his confidence back. 'It can't be too far to the highway.'

'What?' said Phoenix. 'Walk? With no water and no phone! You're crazy.'

'So what do *you* want to do? Sit here and wait to die?' Cameron turned and strode off. 'Let's go. We need to get some miles in before the sun gets too high.'

'What about the sheep?' called Phoenix, running after his brother.

'They're welcome to come if they want to,' grunted Cameron. 'We could do with some lucky mascots now.'

'What did you say mascots were, dear?' asked Sal as the boys hurried away.

'I'm not sure,' replied Wills. 'I think it's something to do with good luck.'

'So if we stick with them, we'll be lucky?' said Oxo.

'And get to this Fort Wilmot place?'

'I think they think *we* bring *them* luck,' said Wills.

But the other Warriors weren't listening. They'd all crowded past him to follow the lucky humans more closely.

They followed for a long time. More than two hours.

'So where's this highway, Cam?' demanded Phoenix.

He was becoming cranky. The burning colours of the desert, the reds, yellows and browns, were beginning to swim before his eyes. He felt that he himself was being melted by the merciless sun. Cameron didn't have the energy to answer. His mouth was too dry anyway.

Phoenix pointed with a wavering hand. 'We've passed that cactus before!'

There were a million cacti. They all looked the same. The Warrior Sheep were still plodding hopefully along behind.

'This good luck thing's taking a while to kick in . . .' muttered Oxo.

'Look!' croaked Sal with sudden excitement. 'Look! Water! A pond! Just ahead there! Just ahead . . .' She staggered into a gallop. 'I can see a pond!'

The pond kept moving away in front of her. It shimmered and glinted in the sunlight, but she could never quite reach it.

'Come back, Sal,' called Wills, forcing himself into a run to catch up with her. 'There is no pond.'

'But I saw it, dear,' sobbed Sal. 'Truly I did . . .'

'It isn't real,' said Wills. 'It's a trick of the light. I think it's called a mirage.'

'Is it, dear?' said Sal vaguely. 'I'm so terribly sorry . . .'

She didn't know what Wills was talking about, but there was no pool of crystal clear water. The other sheep gathered around.

'Hey, man,' said Links. 'Tell me *that's* a mirage tingy too.'

They all looked where he was looking and saw a skeleton of sun-bleached bones lying on the sand close by. Wills shook his head.

'Er, no. Not a mirage,' he said.

'Bones,' grunted Oxo. 'Sheep-sized.'

'Ohmygrass . . .' whimpered Jaycey. 'Red Tongue's been here . . .'

The Warriors looked around anxiously, but the only other living creatures they could see were Cameron and Phoenix, staggering on ahead of them. Then, when it seemed things couldn't possibly get worse, they did.

At first, the breeze was refreshing. Hot but pleasant. It came in little gusts, blowing in the sheep's faces and ruffling their fleeces. Quickly though, the gusts grew stronger and the pauses between each one shorter. Soon, tufts of spiky grass were being ripped up and bowled along the ground. The sun was blotted out and the sheep felt a hot breath on their fleeces.

'Nooo . . .' wailed Jaycey. 'He'scominghe'scoming-he'scoming!'

The breath grew fiercer. The sheep drew closer together. Through half-closed eyes, they could just see Cameron and Phoenix stumbling against the suddenly savage wind.

'The wind!' exclaimed Sal. 'We are where the hottest winds blow! The prophecy is confirmed!'

'Great to know, man . . . great to know . . .' murmured Links.

The hot breath became a howling, blistering gale,

whipping up the sand so that their eyes, noses and mouths were swiftly and completely clogged. The humans and then the entire world around the sheep disappeared in a gritty, stinging haze. The Warriors had no choice. As one, they turned their backs to the sand storm and hunkered down as close to the ground as they could get.

Gradually, the storm eased. The wind dropped to a breeze again and finally that died away too. Five mounds of storm-driven sand began to move. Five pairs of yellow eyes peered out at the great balls of tumbleweed rolling by in the fading wind. Oxo broke free of his sand hill and snapped hungrily at one of the balls.

'I wouldn't bother, man.' Links' voice came from a neighbouring mound. 'They's just organic barbed wire.'

'So what's not to like?' asked Oxo, who was rather partial to barbed wire, as long as it was crisp and rusty.

But the tumbleweed proved just as tough and dry and tasteless as everything else he'd tried in the desert. He chewed his own fleece for a bit instead, and blamed Red Tongue for everything, which made him feel better.

Having realised that the storm was over, the other Warriors were shaking themselves free of the sand. One by one they stood up, coughing and sneezing. Then the sun reappeared, blazing down on them once more from the harsh blue sky. The silence was as thick as the dust on the Warriors' fleeces. Too weary to speak, they spluttered and choked and plodded on. They'd only gone twenty paces west, however, when they heard a feeble cry behind them.

'Hey, guys, wait for us . . .'

Turning, they realised they'd forgotten the humans.

Phoenix and Cameron struggled to their feet, wheezing and wiping sand from their faces. They swayed as they tried to follow the sheep. After a few stumbling paces, Cameron sank to the ground again and rolled on his back, staring at the sky. Phoenix knelt beside him, his own head spinning.

'Sorry, Phee . . .' Cameron's voice was a whisper. 'We're gonna die and it's all my fault . . .'

Phoenix looked wildly, helplessly around. He knew Cameron was right. They needed water fast. They needed a miracle.

The sheep plodded back and clustered around,

blinking. They all felt dizzy and weak. Dark shadows circling on the sand made Jaycey dizzier than ever.

'Ohmygrass . . .' she whimpered. 'What's that?'

Squinting upwards, they saw two large, gliding birds with black feathers, bald heads and curved beaks.

'Vultures,' croaked Wills. 'They're waiting.'

'What for?' asked Oxo.

'For us to die,' answered Wills.

11
Sal's Ear

Wills knew from the cowboy films he'd watched with Tod that vultures live on dead meat. It wasn't a nice thought. He glanced up again. They were still there, circling, watching.

Sal suddenly wobbled and lurched sideways.

'What's up now?' croaked Oxo. 'Have you had another mirage?'

'It's my ear,' said Sal, lurching even further. 'It's buzzing again.'

'Ohmygrass . . .' Jaycey gasped as she stared.

Sal's ear was sticking straight out from her head and pulling Sal with it. She stumbled and fell, her neck outstretched.

'Sal, Sal, get up!' cried Jaycey. 'The vulture birds will think you're dead and rip you to bits and then you will be dead and you're not dead so getupgetupgetup!'

The buzzing was louder now. Wills suddenly realised what it could mean. He remembered the flood.

'Dig,' he cried. 'Dig!'

'What for?' asked Oxo.

'Just dig,' Wills urged. 'Here, by Sal's head.'

He started to scrape at the hard dirt. They all joined in, and slowly the dust-dry ground beneath their hooves became heavier and stonier. Oxo drove his head into the hollow they'd created and his nose came out wet.

'Water!' he coughed. 'There's water down here!'

They dug deeper, faster, and tiny puddles of moisture began to join together, forming a bigger puddle. Sal's ear finally stopped quivering.

The sheep leaned over the puddle in turns and lapped a little of the cool, clean water.

'The humans now,' said Wills.

Phoenix had seen and was trying to speak.

'Cam . . . Cam . . .' he rasped. 'They've found water . . .'

Still on his knees, he tried to drag his brother across the dirt. The Warriors came to meet him and, by gently butting and nudging, did their best to help.

Phoenix scooped up water from the hole and splashed it on Cameron's face. Then, heaving him into a sitting position, he trickled water between his brother's lips before leaning over and sucking in a mouthful himself. Then the Warriors took it in turns again and this time, as water bubbled up from somewhere way below the surface, they drank their fill. When they'd finally had enough, they stood in a circle around Sal, their faces dripping. Her ear and the stud in it were still and quiet.

'Respect, man,' said Links, tapping a hoof against Sal's shoulder. 'How did you know it was there?'

Sal looked modestly at the ground. 'I suppose it's because I'm in touch with my inner sheepliness,' she said. 'Being able to sense the presence of water must have been so useful to our ancestors.'

'Not in Eppingham,' objected Jaycey with a frown.

'Cool though,' said Oxo. 'Couldn't sense the presence of a few fat cauliflowers as well, could you?'

Sal merely beamed at the Warriors. 'We all have powers long since forgotten,' she declared.

Wills wondered if it had more to do with silver studs applied with staple guns, but he said nothing. And if he was right, then there was another question: why had the Staple Gun Woman tagged Sal to find water? And what was Oxo's gold stud for?

Wills glanced across at the boys. They had water now, but Cameron was shivering despite the heat. He looked really ill and Phoenix didn't look much better. Clearly, they could't walk and they were too big for the sheep to carry. But the Warriors couldn't just leave them. The vultures had drifted away but they would be back.

Wills scanned the empty landscape, hoping to see the dust of a vehicle. Nothing. Then, above the rim of the far-off mountains, he saw a speck in the sky.

Phoenix had seen it too.

'Helicopter . . .' he croaked. 'Cam . . . there's a helicopter!'

The chop and whine of the rotors gradually became audible in the still desert air, although the machine was a long way off. Was it searching or just passing?

'Guys, we've got to attract its attention!' cried Wills.

He began running backwards and forwards.

'Oh dear,' sighed Sal. 'It's really too hot for this.'

But she and the others joined Wills, running up and down and bleating loudly.

High above, the helicopter pilot saw movement to his left. As he dipped his machine towards it, he saw what seemed to be a small flock of super-charged sheep. He turned to the paramedic beside him. Her eyes were even wider than his. Then she pointed.

The sheep had to turn their backs as the landing helicopter created another sand storm. Then, once the rotors had slowed, they trotted to where Phoenix and Cameron were lying. The paramedic ran towards them and crouched beside the humans.

'Are you Phoenix and Cameron Dinsdale?' she asked.

Phoenix managed a nod.

'Your mom reported you missing. We've been searching since dawn.' She glanced at the puddle. 'We were expecting to find a couple of corpses.'

The pilot joined her, bringing a stretcher, and between them they carried Cameron quickly to the helicopter. When they came back for Phoenix, he was on his feet, wavering but determined.

'You've gotta take these guys as well,' he said. 'Wherever you're going. They saved our lives – twice. We're not moving without them.'

The paramedic shrugged.

'OK,' she said. 'I guess we can take them back to Fort Wilmot.'

Wills had heard the words 'Fort Wilmot'.

'It's a Red Tongue place, remember?' he said urgently to the other sheep.

And the pilot had no sooner lowered the helicopter's ramp than the Warriors were scampering onboard.

'Is that another car?' asked Oxo, peering from the helicopter's open doorway, while they waited for the paramedic to strap her human patients in safely.

'Ohmygrass . . .' Jaycey was standing beside him. 'It's staplegunwoman . . .'

Holly Boomberg screeched to a halt, well away from the whirring rotor blades, and leapt from her golf buggy.

'You can't take those sheep!' she yelled, spotting Oxo in the doorway. 'They're mine!'

97

But none of the humans heard her above the noise.

'Ready for lift off,' shouted the pilot, and the paramedic slammed the door shut as the helicopter rose from the ground and whirled away.

Down on the ground, however, spitting sand between gritted teeth, Holly was already back behind the wheel of her buggy. She'd read the words on the side of the helicopter:

AIR AMBULANCE FORT WILMOT

Just after dawn at Back of Beyond Ranch, Tod and Gran had woken cold and thirsty by the dying embers of their fire. Tod threw on some more sticks until it flared again.

'I'm going to try and make some smoke signals, Gran,' he said. 'To attract someone's attention.'

Gran creaked to her feet.

'Good idea,' she said, then gave him a little nudge. 'I hope you spell better with smoke than you do with a pencil.' She walked stiffly towards the door. 'While you're doing that, I'll get some water for our imaginary cuppa.'

She picked up her bag, pushed open the door and stepped out into the harsh light of the yard. And the twin barrels of a shotgun.

12
The Sheriff of Gunslinger City

The man holding the gun was huge. He was tall and upright, with broad shoulders and a leathery, tanned face. He wore cowboy boots and a fancy waistcoat, and stared down at Gran from the shade of a stetson hat. Pinned to the breast of his waistcoat was a sheriff's badge.

'Howdy, ma'am,' he said to Gran, lowering the gun only a little.

'Hallelujah!' cried Gran. 'How did you know we were here?'

'I've been watching your smoke all night,' said the sheriff. 'Fires ain't permitted in this territory. Could I ask what you're doing here?'

Tod was standing beside his gran.

'We're looking for our sheep,' he began. 'And . . .'

'Uh-huh.' The sheriff was still pointing the gun.

'And what sheep would that be, exactly?'

'The Eppingham Rare Breeds.'

'Is that so?' The sheriff nodded but he didn't sound as if he believed a word. 'Could I ask you to empty that bag, please, ma'am?'

Gran hesitated, then upended her bag. The contents of the bottomless pit cascaded out on to the ground. The sheriff surveyed the resultant untidy pyramid of bath plugs, head torches, sticky tape, clothes pegs and loo rolls; then he stepped forward and poked it warily with his shotgun.

'You good people got I.D.?' he enquired.

'I'm Ida White and this is my great-grandson Tod.'

'Not names, ma'am. I.D. Proof.'

Tod and Gran looked at each other, then at the jumble of bag contents.

'Oh dear,' said Gran. 'I must have left our passports in Mr Rhubarb's car.'

The sheriff nodded. It was the same style of nod he'd used before.

'Mr Rhubarb's car . . .' he repeated thoughtfully. Then he waved the gun at Tod. 'Go put that fire out, boy, and come straight back.'

Tod went quickly into the ranch house.

'You can restack your bag, ma'am,' continued the sheriff. He watched while she rammed the contents back in, then added, 'By the way, you're under arrest.'

'You're arresting the wrong people!' cried Tod, stamping on the remains of the fire. 'We've been kidnapped and dumped here. He said he wanted to keep us out of the way until B-Day. But we haven't got a phone to contact the police.'

The sheriff gave him another disbelieving look. 'Then I guess you'll have to make do with me, son. The name's Tiny. On account of I ain't. And I'm the sheriff of Gunslinger City. Can you ride?'

Tod and Gran nodded and the sheriff looked towards the sagging gate, where a huge white horse and a small brown mule were tethered.

'You can share the mule,' he said.

Tod helped Gran on to the mule, then hoisted himself into the saddle behind her. There was just room for both of them. The sheriff looked down at them from the comfort of his own beautifully decorated leather saddle.

'This is Lightning,' he said, patting the horse's neck. 'You ever been to Gunslinger City?'

Tod and Gran shook their heads.

'Well then,' said Sheriff Tiny, jerking the mule's tether free of the gate and leading his captives away. 'Your day's about to get even better.'

The horse and mule walked steadily through the desert for some time. Nobody spoke. Tod's mind was racing. Should he try to escape? Should he try to fight? Should he try to explain again about Rhubarb and the sheep? He glanced up at the sheriff's stern face. And at the gun. He decided to keep quiet for a bit. The mule stopped abruptly to tear at a cactus plant and Tod had to hang on tight to stop himself and Gran falling off. He would wait until they got to Gunslinger. Surely there would be someone there who would believe their story?

The sun was getting higher and hotter when the sheriff eventually announced, 'Here we are, folks. Gunslinger City.'

'It's just a ghost town,' said Gran as they jolted down the main street.

High on his white horse, Sheriff Tiny flinched

slightly. What the old lady said was true, but it hurt him to hear it.

'My great-great-gran'pappy was sheriff here in the Gold Rush,' he said proudly. 'There was a lotta gold found hereabouts. Gunslinger was one heck of a place then. Full of miners, traders, saloon girls . . .'

'That's history,' said Gran. 'It's a ghost town.'

She was still angry at being arrested, and didn't care about the sheriff's great-great-gran'pappy.

'You can't say it don't look real enough,' said Tiny. He nodded at the general store, the chapel, the hotel and the saloon as they passed.

'There are no people,' said Gran.

'There will be. The first bus'll be arriving in half an hour. We can get upwards of five hundred folk a day.'

This was true as well, but Tiny took no real satisfaction from it. A hundred and fifty years ago, Gunslinger had been on the cattle trail and the gold trail. Now, it was on the tourist trail; it had a café and a gift shop. As sheriff, his time was mostly spent directing people to the washrooms or posing for photographs. Today though, he'd made a genuine arrest. He intended to make the most of it.

Tiny reined in outside the jail house, dismounted and tethered his horse and the mule to the hitching rail. Tod jumped down and helped Gran. At any other time, he would have been thrilled to be here. It was like being in the actual Wild West.

As Tod looked around, Gran suddenly made a break for it.

'Run, Tod!' she cried, ducking away, but the sheriff took just one step, stretched out a long arm and grabbed her.

'That's resisting arrest, lady,' he said disapprovingly.

'Too right,' answered Gran, wriggling and kicking.

To be on the safe side, Tiny grabbed Tod with his other hand and with one squirming prisoner tucked under each arm, stepped on to the boardwalk.

'I want to speak to your boss!' yelled Tod. 'The Marshal or the Mayor or someone!'

The sheriff merely tightened his grip, barged open the door to the jail house and strode inside. Passing through a small office, he kicked open the cell door and dropped Tod and Gran on the floor. Gran swung at him with her bag, but Tiny dodged the blow.

'Easy now . . .' he warned.

He clanged the cell door shut. Tod rushed at it and rattled the bars as Tiny turned and removed the key.

'You can't do this!' Tod shouted.

'I just did, boy.'

'But we're not criminals!'

'Of course not,' agreed Tiny with a disbelieving smile. 'You're friends of Mr Rhubarb. Now you just let me know when you wanna start talking sense.'

And he turned away and strolled out, taking the cell key with him.

13

Snorting Sam

Fort Wilmot was a big town with an airport, a railway station and a lot of wide, busy roads. There was no sign of Red Tongue, though, and the Warriors weren't sure what to do next as the helicopter landed outside the hospital.

When the engine was switched off and the sheep's ear protectors had been removed, Wills heard the paramedic speak again.

'Where did you dumb kids think you were going, anyhow?' she asked.

'Here,' said Phoenix, trying to stand up. 'Fort Wilmot. D'you think we'll be able to see the Rams tonight? When they go head to head with Red Tongue?'

'No way,' said the paramedic.

'But we'll be fine by then,' protested Phoenix as Wills shifted closer to listen.

What rams did they mean, he wondered? Oxo and Links? The paramedic gave Wills a pat.

'You know,' she said, 'I reckon these sheep are brighter than you guys. You get lost in the desert with no water, no phone, no radio. And you get your dates wrong too. Red Tongue slaughtered the Rams here *last* night. You missed it. They've moved on. Las Vegas is next.'

She gave Wills a smile and another pat as a hospital team arrived to disembark the humans.

'I'll see if the vet can transplant you an ovine brain cell or two,' she said to the boys. 'That is, if your mom doesn't strangle you first.'

'Look after those sheep,' called Cameron anxiously, to no one in particular, as he was wheeled towards the hospital.

But Wills didn't wait to be looked after by anyone. He led the way down the ramp out of the helicopter.

'We're too late,' he explained unhappily. 'There was a slaughter of rams here last night.'

'Ohmygrass . . .' For once, Jaycey spoke for everyone.

'Respect for the dead, man . . .' murmured Links.

They all looked at their hooves in silence.

'So I think,' said Wills, 'we have to get to a place called Las Vegas now.'

He'd seen a railway line as the helicopter was landing. The Warriors, even Oxo, knew about railways as well as helicopters. They'd been on a train once, though only in the guard's van. It was time to try again.

Wills found a green man and crossed a road, then saw a sign to the railway station. The only problem was that it directed the sheep down a side street full of houses. Each house had a low white fence. And inside each fence was a well-watered lawn. After the desert experience, the temptation was too much.

'Feed the fleece to fight the foe!' cried Sal.

Oxo didn't need telling twice. He skipped over the first fence and got his head down in the life-giving greenery. The noise of juicy ripping soon had the other sheep, even Wills, following his example.

'Keep moving,' called Wills, between stuffed mouthfuls. 'Eat on the hoof.'

So the Warriors shuffled through the gardens like four-legged lawn mowers.

When they finally reached the station car park,

Wills saw a poster with a picture of a strange-looking train.

ALL ABOARD SNORTING SAM!
FORT WILMOT TO GRAND CANYON AND BACK
JUMP OFF FOR LAS VEGAS

In the distance beyond the station, he heard a loud, slightly mournful whistle.

'Guys!' he called urgently. 'I think there's a train coming!'

The others dragged themselves away from their lawns and followed as Wills hurried towards the station and squeezed through a gateway on to the platform. A large crowd of people was already waiting, chatting excitedly, craning their necks to catch a first glimpse of the oncoming train.

'Here he comes, Junior,' said a man, hoisting a little boy up on to his shoulders.

'Is it Snorting Sam?' asked the boy excitedly.

'The real deal,' his dad assured him.

The whistle blew again and a huge cloud of smoke belched from the funnel as the train clanked into the station. It was a very old steam locomotive, with big wheels, high carriages, lots of shiny brass and a huge metal scoop fixed to the front.

'That's a cow catcher,' the dad said to Junior. 'They used to scoop away critters that strayed on to the rails.'

The driver was standing on the footplate, pulling on the brake. He waved to the waiting passengers as the giant wheels ground to a halt. Beside him, sweat streaming down his coal-blackened face, the stoker leaned on his shovel in front of the open furnace. At the very back of the train, there was an open platform with a thick brass rail around it.

People clambered eagerly up the steps into the carriages and found their seats. Junior's dad made his way to the back, to the viewing platform, and stood leaning against the rail with his son.

'Let's follow him,' said Wills. 'We won't be so noticeable out there.'

He'd remembered something about needing tickets. The sheep squeezed through and stood on the viewing platform, trying to look as if they weren't there.

'This is so much nicer than the last train we were on,' said Sal approvingly.

'Yeah,' said Links. 'Everything in America's more modern, innit.'

The whistle screeched, jets of steam hissed out on to the platform, and the wheels began to turn. Junior waved excitedly and the train chugged out of the station.

'Who brought the woollies?'

A ticket inspector had appeared in the carriage next to the viewing platform. Everyone shrugged and looked at everyone else.

'Aw, they're not doing any harm,' called Junior's dad. 'Let 'em come for the ride.'

The inspector shrugged. 'OK,' he said. 'I'll give 'em a sheep day return.'

He laughed, pleased with his joke, and slapped a ticket on Sal's broad back.

The Warriors settled to chew the cud and look out at the scenery rushing past. The last of the desert soon gave way to fields, then forest, as the train climbed higher and higher. Soon, all they could see were pine trees on either side.

An old man wearing a stetson hat and carrying a banjo came and sat in the carriage next to the viewing platform.

'Howdy, folks,' he said. 'Y'all enjoying the ride?'

Everyone said they were.

He strummed the banjo. 'I'll soon put a stop to that.'

Everyone laughed.

'A few things I have to tell you first. When we arrive at the Canyon, there'll be a bus waiting for those going straight on to Vegas. Don't be late. The bus won't wait.' He strummed a few more chords on his banjo. 'Las Vegas . . . Funny kind of name for the place, ain't it? It's Spanish: means "The Meadows".'

Everyone laughed again, but Wills didn't understand why.

'Meadows? What? As in grassy fields?' asked Oxo eagerly when Wills told the others what the banjo man had said.

'Got to be, man,' said Links. 'Meadows have sheep, innit. That's why Red Tongue's goin' there. To carry on the slaughtering ting.'

So Oxo shut up about meadows. But then the

old man with the banjo strummed a bit more and started singing.

'Oh, I'm a lonesome cowboy, and I'm a long, long way from home . . .'

Links hunched his shoulders. 'Man . . . where's the ear protectors when you really need them?'

The rest of the Warriors weren't so fussy. In fact, they all enjoyed the music.

'Oh, Su-sannah . . .' sang the human passengers.

'Baa . . . baa . . . ba-ba . . .' bleated the sheep.

'Don't you cry for me . . .!'

'Ba, ba, ba, ba, ba . . .!'

'For I'm goin' to Grand Canyon with a sheep right on my knee!'

They were all still singing when the train finally clackety-clacked to a halt. Wills watched as most of the passengers hurried excitedly away from the station.

'They're going to see the Canyon,' he said wistfully. 'I wonder if we've got time?'

'Don't be late, the bus won't wait,' chanted Jaycey primly. She could see it in the car park.

'What is this Grand Canyon ting, anyway?' asked Links as the rest of the sheep followed Jaycey.

'It's like a valley,' said Wills. 'But massive.'

'What, bigger than Soggy Bottom?' said Oxo disbelievingly.

Soggy Bottom was the valley in Eppingham where they sometimes went for a change of grass.

'Much bigger,' said Wills. 'I saw it on Tod's TV. It's miles wide and deep and it gets so hot and dry in summer that hardly anything can live there.'

'So . . . correct me if I'm wrong,' said Oxo, 'but you're saying this Canyon thing is just a hot, dusty hole in the ground. With no grub?'

'A special hole,' insisted Wills.

But he'd already lost their attention. Jaycey and Sal had come to a halt beside the parked bus. The doors were open and the driver was asleep behind the wheel.

'Is this the one we want, dear?' asked Sal.

The driver snored loudly and shifted about in his seat.

'Yes,' Wills whispered, reading the sign on the front. 'It's going to Las Vegas. Better sneak on quietly though. It says "No Pets".'

'Pets!' snorted Links. 'Pets is cats and dogs, innit. We's Warriors, man.'

The driver grunted loudly and shifted his weight again.

'Sshhh . . .'

Wills waited for the man to settle and then sprang up the steps and into the bus. He tip-hooved past the driver and ran lightly along the aisle to the back. He'd hoped they could hide behind the seats, but Oxo, Links and Sal were much too big to squash in.

'Perhaps if we sit very still on the back seat, he won't notice us,' murmured Wills.

So they scrambled quietly on to the back seat and sat in a line, facing forward, as if they were part of the bus.

A few people from the train were hurrying across the car park now. The driver heard their trundling suitcases and shook himself awake. He took their money and handed them tickets as they clambered aboard. A few of them nodded at the line of sheep on the back seat. The sheep nodded politely back. They'd become acquainted on the train. The humans settled into their seats and the driver closed the doors.

'Las Vegas only,' he called, without turning in his seat. 'Las Vegas next stop.'

And he drove off without noticing his extra passengers.

A few hours later, the Fort Wilmot hospital doors hissed open and Holly Boomberg strode in. She marched to the reception desk.

'I'm looking for a flock of sheep,' she announced abruptly. 'Where are they?'

The receptionist looked up. She'd developed a way of dealing with rude customers. It was called 'being rude back'.

'This is a hospital, lady,' she said. 'The H is for humans.'

Holly clenched her fists. And her teeth.

'They arrived by air ambulance earlier today,' she said. 'I *know* they did.'

'Try the veterinary centre across the park,' suggested the receptionist, no longer looking at her. 'We don't do sheep.'

'We saw some, didn't we, Dad?'

The voice behind her made Holly spin round. A small boy was sitting on a chair beside his father. He'd fallen over and cut his knee when jumping down from a train, and was bravely waiting to be stitched.

'Sure did, Junior,' said his dad.

'Where?' snapped Holly. 'How many?'

'There were five,' said Junior, still excited. 'On Snorting Sam. Then they got on the bus to Vegas. They were real cute.'

'Sure were,' said his dad.

Holly was already on her way out. The doors hissed shut behind her as she jabbed fiercely at her phone. Eventually, her husband answered. 'Hi, honey,' he said cheerfully.

He was back at base now, surrounded by computers and people in white coats who called him 'sir'. He'd completely forgotten Tod and Ida.

'Stanley, I'm going to Las Vegas,' his wife snapped.

'Vegas?' Stanley tried not to snap back. What was she talking about now? 'This is no time for a vacation, honey.'

In the background an automated voice was chiming down the seconds: Ninety-two thousand, one hundred and fifteen . . .

'Can you hear that?' demanded the Professor. 'The

countdown? Tomorrow *is* B-Day, remember. Where are my sheep?'

'Stanley.' Holly's voice was sharp. 'Shut up and catch a plane. Your sheep are in Las Vegas. Meet me there. I need your help.'

She switched off her phone and drove her golf buggy to the airport.

'*You* need *my* help?' muttered the Professor to his silent phone.

For a moment the surprising thought pleased him, but then he remembered the countdown again and began to panic.

Tod and Ida's cell in Gunslinger City was clean and cool, with a dirt floor and white painted walls. There were two bunk beds, a chair and a little stove with a pile of logs beside it. A door in one corner led to a tiny toilet cubicle. There was no window, but plenty of daylight from the sheriff's office and the street beyond. And the prisoners were not alone.

All day, they'd been rattling their cell bars and pleading with the tourists who wandered in and out of the jail house. None had taken them seriously.

'Great act,' the man now standing by the sheriff's desk called. 'You sure look like the real thing. Wild Boy Billy and Granny Gunsmoke.'

'We are not an act!' shouted Tod for the hundredth time. 'We're not even American. We're prisoners!'

The people in the jail house laughed and clapped.

'Well done, son,' said the man as he turned to go. 'You've got a great future in the movies.'

The rest of the group followed him out, chuckling. Tod sighed and turned to Gran.

'It's beginning to get dark,' he said. 'There won't be any more visitors now. We'll have to try again tomorrow.'

Gran was looking thoughtful.

'Is Sheriff Half Wit out there?' she asked.

Tod peered through the bars.

'I can't see him. Why? Did you want more food?'

They'd eaten the Gunslinger Gumbo that Tiny had brought them earlier.

'No,' said Ida. 'Help me move the bunk.'

Tod looked at her, then dragged one corner of the bunk beds away from the wall. The floor behind it seemed a little less firm.

'It's worth a try,' said Gran.

She picked up the little shovel that stood by the stove and handed it to Tod.

'Get digging!'

14
The Meadows

Sitting on the back seat of the bus, heading for Las Vegas, the Warrior Sheep were thinking of only one thing: Red Tongue.

'We're gonna have to be cunning, innit,' Links was saying. 'He must be quick on his feet the way he keeps movin'. Brute force won't be enough.'

'Will be when *I* catch him,' growled Oxo.

Jaycey yawned. 'What do you think, Wills?'

But for once Wills couldn't offer guidance. Exhausted by his efforts in getting them this far, he'd fallen asleep.

'Such a lambkin,' sniffed Jaycey.

But very soon she was nodding too. And so were the others. The bus drove steadily through the desert with its load of dozing people and sheep. The sun set and stars began to twinkle in the dark night sky.

High above them, a plane began its descent into Las Vegas airport.

'Wakey-wakey, folks,' was the next thing the sheep heard. 'Welcome to Las Vegas! Wakey-wakey!'

The Warriors followed the human passengers to the front of the bus and waited their turn to get off. The driver was in mid-yawn when he noticed them. He finally shut his mouth then opened it again, blinking as he did so.

'When did you guys get on?' he demanded.

But the sheep were already jumping down from the bus into a hot Las Vegas night.

The sky was darkest blue-black, but everywhere lights blazed and danced and twinkled. The bus had stopped in the main street, outside the biggest building the Warriors had ever seen. Except maybe for the building next door to it. Every building on the street was enormous and they were all pulsing with coloured lights and neon signs. Fountains sent jets of water almost as high as the buildings themselves, and thousands of people surged in and out of the open doorways. The Warriors stood in a cluster, staring around, bewildered.

Jaycey was the first to speak. 'Ohmygrass . . . it's . . . it's fleecetastic . . .'

Oxo was less impressed. He'd woken up looking forward to a quick snack.

'Funny kind of meadows,' he grunted. 'I can't see a blade of grass anywhere.'

Just then the ground beneath his hooves began to move. The sheep looked down. They were standing on a silvery metal strip that stretched from the pavement to the nearest huge building. And it was indeed moving, drawing them slowly past slanting glass walls towards an enormous doorway.

'Whoa, man,' cried Links. 'Where we goin'?'

Wills looked up at the glittering sign above the doorway and read aloud as they glided beneath it.

'Hotel English Meadows.'

A huge fountain in the centre of the reception lobby shot jets of purple and green water high into the air. Gentle music played and slot machines around the walls jingled and flashed. The space was filled with people: visitors with suitcases, coming and going, waiters dressed like shepherds, carrying trays of food, musicians in old-fashioned costumes, playing flutes, and girls in long skirts and bonnets, handing out flowers.

'Well, at least it's nice and cool,' said Sal, thankfully.

Jaycey sighed again, starry-eyed. 'It's just . . .'

'Fleecetastic,' grunted Oxo. 'You already told us.'

He'd just tried a nibble of the grass-green floor and discovered it was made of plastic.

A girl in a floaty pink dress bent and tucked a flower into Jaycey's fleece.

'You are sooo cute,' she said, before strolling away.

Then a waiter in a shepherd's smock offered Jaycey a lettuce leaf from the silver tray on his arm. 'Hey, you're pretty,' he said.

'I want to stay here for ever and ever . . .' breathed Jaycey.

Oxo just spat out shreds of plastic.

Jaycey had forgotten about Red Tongue. She'd forgotten about Tod and Ida and Eppingham. She'd even forgotten about Sal and Wills and Links and Oxo. So when a hand with lots of diamond rings and bangles tickled her under the chin, and its owner said, 'You're *beautiful*. Do you want to come for a little walk?', she followed the woman in the long blue dress and glittering jewels to the lift.

'You need to freshen up a bit, cutie,' the woman said. 'I can fix that.'

The lift doors opened and the woman swept in with Jaycey at her heels. The other sheep looked round.

'Jaycey! Come back!' they all yelled, and they galloped towards the lift.

The doors hissed shut in their faces.

15
Gambolling in Las Vegas

As Jaycey was disappearing into the lift, Professor Stanley Boomberg was appearing in the Arrivals Hall at Las Vegas airport. He'd had a short doze on the plane but felt worse for it. It *was* the night before B-Day, after all. He shouldn't be hurrying to meet his wife in Las Vegas of all places. Panic had given way to sheer bad temper. And people were staring at him for some reason.

Holly was there waiting. Impatiently. She'd had a short nap on her plane too, but felt refreshed and ready for action. She stepped forward when she saw Stanley and took the pencils out of his ears. She so wished he wouldn't do that in public. Even a genius looked silly with pencils in his ears.

'What's gone wrong, honey?' asked the Professor as his wife thrust the pencils roughly into the breast pocket of his white coat.

'Nothing's gone wrong,' said Holly shortly, wishing also that he would remember to take his white coat off when he left his laboratory. 'But I knew you'd be fretting, so I wanted you with me. It's called teamwork.'

It was also called sharing the blame but she wasn't going to admit that.

'We *are* dealing with the most extraordinary creatures in the universe,' she added.

Stanley was beginning to wonder if he really did want them. Time was running out and he would make do with any old sheep. Even a couple of rats. But Holly didn't give him the chance to say so. She turned and walked briskly away.

'Did you leave the crone and her kid at Back of Beyond Ranch?' she asked over her shoulder. 'Like I told you to?'

Stanley stared blankly for a moment, then remembered the old lady and the boy. He decided against telling the truth.

'Yes,' he said, following her. 'They won't cause us any bother.'

'Good.' Holly strode on towards the taxi rank.

'So, have you located your extraordinary sheep again, honey?' asked the Professor, trying to keep up. 'You do know exactly where they are?'

'Of course.' It was Holly's turn to lie now.

The Professor looked around. 'I don't see them.'

Holly clicked her fingers at the nearest taxi driver. 'Stanley, they're highly intelligent animals,' she said, climbing into the cab. 'They use helicopters and buses. There's only one place in town they'd dream of staying.'

Wills and the others rode up and down in the lifts, looking for Jaycey. They trotted along endless corridors and peeped into hundreds of bedrooms. Back on the ground floor, they came to a door guarded by men in black suits. Wills read the notice on the door out loud.

'Serious Gamblers Only.'

'Gambolling's what lambs do, innit?' said Links, puzzled.

'Yeah,' said Oxo. 'Gambolling's jumping up and down in a field. How can you be serious about that?'

They shrugged and pushed past the men in black suits. The people inside weren't jumping up and down. They were sitting at huge round tables: watching cards being turned over or staring at little balls whizzing around black and red dishes. They all looked very serious indeed. The Warriors wriggled their way past their legs to peer under the tables, but there was no sign of Jaycey. They hurried back to the entrance lobby.

'This place is too big,' sighed Sal, plonking herself down on the floor. 'We're never going to find her.'

'Not a good place to sit, ma'am,' said a waiter sweeping past with a huge tray full of drinks. 'You guys probably want the thirty-fifth floor.'

He hurried on.

'We do?' said Sal.

They trotted to the lift and another waiter helpfully tapped the call pad.

'Nice to have you with us,' he said as he leaned in and pressed button thirty-five.

The lift went all the way up in one zoom. It was very fast and arrived at the thirty-fifth floor before most of the Warriors' stomachs. They waited a few seconds for them to catch up, then got out.

'Well, butt my butt!' said Oxo, staring.

It was as if they'd been transported back to England. Eppingham, even. But without the rain. They were standing in a sunlit meadow of real, lush grass. Above their heads, white clouds scudded across a blue sky, and in front of them a small flock of sheep, real sheep, grazed peacefully.

'Well, butt my butt too . . .' said Links.

Meanwhile, outside in the real world, a taxi pulled up in front of the Hotel English Meadows. Holly Boomberg thrust some money into the driver's hand, then she and Stanley ran along the metal travellator. The large hotel map in the lobby told Holly what she wanted to know.

'Rural Paradise,' she snapped. 'Come on.'

She hurried Stanley into the nearest lift and pushed the button for the thirty-fifth floor.

'But if the hotel keep a flock up here,' said the Professor as they rode up, 'how are we going to know which two are ours?'

'The sensors in their ears, darling,' said his wife shortly.

But still the thirty-fifth floor came as a bit of a shock.

'I don't believe it!' muttered Holly. 'Why are there so *many* wool bags? I can't even *see* ours.'

'Wonderful, ain't it,' said a waiter, placing a fruit drink in her hand, as he passed. 'Peace and quiet under a blue sky, any time you want it, day or night.' He laughed. 'It's all done with lights and mirrors, but enjoy.'

He stepped into a lift and the doors slid shut.

Holly turned back to the sheep and took a length of rope from her briefcase. She'd just caught a glint of artificial sunlight reflecting off the gold stud in Oxo's ear.

'Follow me, Stanley,' she said. 'Quietly . . .'

The Warriors were talking earnestly to the hotel sheep and didn't notice the two humans sneaking towards them.

'It's all there in the Songs of the Fleece,' Sal was saying. 'The beast will eat us all unless we stop it.'

'Red Tongue's the name,' said Oxo. 'You've got to get out while you can.'

'Yeah, yeah . . .' said one of the grazing sheep.

'We never go out,' said another.

They continued grazing.

'And then there's Jaycey, innit,' said Links urgently. 'A little black-and-white Jacob. Stupid but nice. Have you seen her?'

'Nope.' The grazers went on grazing.

Wills glanced up and saw Holly.

'Look out, Sal!' he cried. 'It's Staple Gun Woman!'

Holly lunged but Sal jumped out of the way and the rope missed. Stanley, meanwhile, had been told to target Oxo.

'Got you!' he cried.

He threw himself at the big ram just as the lift doors opened and a crowd of people wandered out on to the real grass, exclaiming in delight at the rural paradise of peace in which they found themselves.

Wills saw the Warriors' chance.

'Run!' he yelled.

He raced for the open lift with Links and Sal close behind. Oxo twisted and heaved and charged after them, with the thin man who'd tried to capture him being dragged across the grass, still clinging to his wool. Oxo turned his head to bite, but the man let go and rolled into the crowd of newly arrived humans.

The sudden noise and drama had panicked the

hotel sheep in a way the Warriors' dire warnings had failed to, and they ran as well. They bundled, bleating and shaking, into the lift after Oxo and the rest, and the door slid shut. It was probably the record number of sheep ever in a lift.

'What is that woman's problem?' gasped Oxo angrily, poking his nose above the mass of woolly backs.

'She's crazy, innit,' said Links.

'Can we get out soon, please?' Wills' voice was a muffled squeak from somewhere at sheep knee height. 'I can't breathe.'

The doors opened and the bundle of baaing sheep tumbled out. There was no time to discuss where to go next. The bell on the second lift dinged. Its door opened and Staple Gun Woman and her man burst out, followed by the entire crowd of people from the thirty-fifth floor.

With Oxo in the lead, the Warriors galloped off down the nearest corridor and the hotel sheep followed. They skidded around corners and clattered down stairways. Staple Gun Woman and her man kept close behind, and more and more people joined the chase, until a huge mass of shouting, laughing humans were racing after them. Most thought it was another type of hotel entertainment laid on for the guests.

Oxo had no idea where he was going. He was running blindly. He burst into the entrance lobby and crashed into a waiter, then another, then another. Silver trays flew from their hands, showering drinks, sandwiches, fruit and flowers on the floor, where they were trampled to a soggy mess.

Oxo saw the fountain too late. He didn't have time to go around it. He ploughed straight through, stepping on the nozzles as he went. Jets of water squirted and spurted around the lobby. People screamed, laughed and skidded on the slippery floor. Some raced on after the sheep, whooping and yelling.

From the corner of one eye, Oxo suddenly saw a narrow doorway tucked away on the side of the lobby. He changed direction, charged through it and shuddered to a halt.

He was trapped on a narrow landing, staring down a steep, spiral staircase. The rest of the Warriors hurtled in after him and Oxo had to brace his feet on the concrete floor to stop himself being pitched down the stairs.

The hotel sheep didn't try to follow. They milled about on the lobby side of the doorway, exhausted, terrified and unsure what to do, having forgotten why they were doing it anyway.

Holly Boomberg started shoving them roughly aside. She was looking straight through at Sal and Oxo.

'Got you now, my clever little ovines,' she said, re-tying the noose in her rope.

16
The Silver Cage

In the lobby behind the Boombergs, the hotel manager was working to restore order.

'Close the doors,' he commanded into his walkie-talkie radio. 'I want this mess contained!'

Somewhere in a central control department, a button was pressed and all the lobby doors slid silently shut. Holly Boomberg's head banged against the toughened glass with a clunk. Standing at her shoulder, Stanley rather hoped it hurt. He glanced at his wrist computer.

'Honey,' he said urgently, trying to show her his wrist. 'Look at the countdown! These English sheep are way *too* clever. How about we just grab ourselves a couple from the thirty-fifth floor and make do with them?'

Holly pressed her face angrily against the closed

door and hammered with her fists in frustration.

'No!' she said. 'Your great experiment demands the best. These are the best and these you shall have whether you like it or not!'

On the other side, the Warriors blinked at Holly and then turned to peer down the stairwell. The manager's calm voice was now radio broadcasting above the chaos.

'Ladies and gentlemen. On behalf of Hotel English Meadows, I would like to apologise for this little, uh, technical difficulty. For your own comfort and safety, the lobby will be closed until further notice. Why not visit our famous basement theatre, where our fabulous Small Hours Show is about to begin?'

Holly turned and grabbed the manager's arm.

'I don't want to visit the theatre,' she snarled. 'Open this door!'

The manager shook her off as politely as he could.

'That's not a public route, madam. If you don't like the theatre, how about a football game? Red Tongue are playing late at the stadium just a few blocks away. Our public doors will be re-opened very shortly.'

He gave her a tight little smile and stalked off, clicking his fingers at staff, left and right.

The sheep had dithered at the top of the spiral staircase until Wills had said, 'Stairs or Staple Gun woman?'

'No contest,' said Links. 'The stairs. Man, they're not even moving.'

Remembering that they'd once ridden on a moving escalator, the Warriors suddenly felt less afraid. Oxo pushed his way to the front.

'Why are we waiting?' he grunted.

'Backwards! Go backwards!' shouted Wills but it was too late.

Oxo's front hooves went down one steep step but there was no room on it for his back hooves. He toppled sideways and started to bounce. Round and round, spiralling down to the bottom.

'Cool move,' laughed Links, then he flopped on his side and pushed off with his hooves. 'Let's rumble tumble.' And down he went.

Sal followed next and finally Wills.

'Shall we do it again?' asked Oxo as they picked themselves up, but Wills was already looking around. They were now in a corridor.

It was narrow, bare and rather dark, but at the far end was a green lit sign.

'Stage Door,' Wills read aloud.

'What's one of them?' asked Oxo.

Wills shrugged. He didn't know.

'Doors is good, innit,' said Links. 'It might have Jaycey behind it.'

So they continued along the corridor, around another corner and up a short flight of steps. There was more light here, more space, and several doors. Also, the end of a high red curtain. And a noise. Human voices. Lots of them, beyond the curtain. They were chattering eagerly, excited; as if waiting for something.

Wills poked his nose around the edge of the curtain. He could see a dark hall, packed with people. A sudden loud voice boomed in the darkness, making Wills and the other sheep jump.

'Ladies and gentlemen . . . We invite you to sit back, relax and prepare to be amazed. Will you welcome please, the great, the unique, the most beautifully dressed magician in Las Vegas: Madam Gloria Fantutti!'

The great curtain swished aside and Wills had to dodge backwards so as not to be seen. He and the rest of the Warriors were dazzled as the space where the curtain had been was lit up by a pool of brilliant white light.

A woman was standing in the pool of light; a woman wearing a lot of jewellery and a blue dress. She spread her arms and beamed at her audience until everyone had finished clapping and cheering.

'Ladies and gentlemen . . .' she purred into a microphone. 'Tonight, I do indeed intend to amaze you. Tonight you will see magic you have never seen before . . .'

She looked upwards, and a spotlight followed her gaze to where something was dangling from the ceiling. It was a silver cage, covered with a sparkly blue cloth.

There was a drum roll from the orchestra, seated somewhere beyond the spotlights, and the silver cage was lowered towards Madam Fantutti, turning slowly as it came.

'Tonight . . .' she announced, 'before your very eyes I shall saw in half . . . not a beautiful girl – you have seen that before. No, I shall do something much more difficult. Something no one else has ever attempted.'

She reached up and whipped the cloth from the cage. The audience gasped, and so did the Warriors. Because inside, trembling with fright, her fleece powdered with silver glitter, and with a blue bow around her neck, stood Jaycey.

'Tonight, I shall saw in half . . . a sheep!'

17
Rap Stars

Madam Fantutti produced a huge silver sword and stabbed it into the stage, where it stood quivering. Inside her cage, Jaycey quivered too.

'Keep still, you little fleabag,' murmured Madam Fantutti out of the corner of her mouth.

A small silver box was wheeled on to the stage. From it, Madam Fantutti took a large cabbage, which she hurled into the air. As it fell, she pulled the sword from the stage and sliced the cabbage neatly in two. The audience gasped. The watching Warriors gulped.

Two stagehands standing close to the sheep gulped too. They were dressed in black jeans and black sweaters and it was their job to carry the performers' equipment on and off stage between acts.

'Man, I don't think I can watch this,' whispered one of the stagehands.

'Nor me,' whispered her colleague. 'She's crazy. I mean, slicing veg is one thing . . .'

'But what are we going to do?' asked the woman. 'Watch her chop that animal up like a turnip?'

'It was a cabbage.'

'That's so not funny.'

The woman looked down at the sheep watching tensely beside her. Maybe they were next.

Another drum roll drew all eyes back to the stage. Madam Fantutti had turned her attention to the silver box on wheels, tipping it towards her audience and opening the lid.

'As you can see . . .' she said, ' . . . the box is completely empty. And has just room enough for one small sheep . . .'

At that moment, the silver cage dropped lower and Madam Fantutti flipped open its door. A second later, she was holding Jaycey aloft.

'She's perfectly real, as you can see,' she told her audience.

She shoved Jaycey into the silver box and squashed her down, so that she was lying on her stomach with her head and front hooves sticking out of holes in the front of the box and her back hooves sticking out of holes at the back.

'No escape, muttonhead,' sneered Madam Fantutti quietly as she closed the lid. 'It's wriggle-proof.'

She looked up and beamed at the audience, then spun the box on its wheels and seized the sword again.

'What are we waiting for?' growled Oxo but Wills hurriedly stopped him as he made to charge on stage.

'She'll kill you too,' he whispered sharply.

The stagehands were staring at Madam Fantutti. 'We have to do *something* . . .' the woman said.

'Not while she's holding that sword, I'm not,' murmured the man.

Wills suddenly felt someone else arrive beside them. It was the hotel manager.

'Get on there and stop her,' he hissed at the stagehands. 'Get her away from that animal! Get her off stage. And make it look like part of the act.'

He turned his back and put his head in his hands. He knew Madam Fantutti. He was asking the impossible. She was a great magician sometimes. Crazy always. Especially with a sword.

Another drum roll. The stagehands were rooted to the spot, shaking with fear. Wills turned urgently to the Warriors.

'It's down to us,' he whispered. 'We've got to get her away from Jaycey, and without her killing anyone else. We've got to distract her . . . confuse her . . .' He drew a quick breath. 'Links – get out there and sing.'

'And now . . .' Madam Fantutti cried dramatically, holding the sword aloft.

But instead of hearing gasps of frightened anticipation from the audience, she heard giggles. She paused, the sword still in both hands, raised above her head. Glancing sideways, she saw four more sheep galloping on to the stage. They skidded to a halt beside her. The one in front was nodding its curly head and tapping a front hoof. Then it started to bleat in a rhythmic sort of way. The ones behind seemed to be trying to copy it.

'Security!' shrieked Madam Fantutti. 'Get these wool bags out of my act!'

But as she shrieked, Links started to rap.

'Hey, Jaycey girl, though you's pretty in blue,

We want you to know that we love you too.

All that glitter on your fleece might get you dates,

But what about your friends, your Eppingham mates?'

'Fleeced up, fleeced up, fleeced up, fleeced up . . .' sang the sheep behind him, hoping it was a cool counter-rhythm. Links nodded approval.

The sword was too heavy to hold above her head any longer and Madam Fantutti let it drop to her side. The stagehands had stopped shaking and nipped on stage behind her. They grabbed the silver box and shoved it hard, sending it spinning away.

'We's here on a mission, as you well know,

An' we reckon there's still a long way to go,

Red Tongue's out there where the sun is hot,

An' he's an evil dude or have you forgot?'

'Fleeced up, fleeced up, fleeced up, fleeced up . . .'

The audience didn't understand a word, but they were loving every second. They began to tap their feet and clap along. The silver box on wheels, hurtling round the stage pursued by the stagehands and the sword-wielding magician, only added to the fun.

'We need you, Jaycey, we need you real bad,
An' if you ever leave, we's gonna be sad,
So listen up, Jaycey, won't you hear my plea?
Stay with your friends, where we want you to be.'

'Fleeced up, fleeced up, fleeced up, fleeced up . . .'

The audience were going wild now, on their feet, stamping and clapping.

'More!' they yelled. 'More!'

Oxo instantly saw his opportunity and darted from the chorus line. His hard head crashed into Madam Fantutti as she blundered past in pursuit of the box and the stagehands. Her feet slipped from under her, and the sword flew from her hand and slid across the stage. The manager dashed on and grabbed it, while the audience roared their approval and the stagehands picked up Madam Fantutti and carried her off between them, still trying to make it look as if it were all part of the performance.

Oxo charged again, this time at the silver box. It

toppled over and Jaycey scrambled out.

'Ohmygrass . . . ohmygrass . . . ohmythankyouthank youthankyou . . .' she sobbed as she skittered across to join the others, who were still singing.

'We's Rare Breed sheep and we's Warriors too,
An' while we's together, we's got work to do.
Cos we's one for all, an' we's all for one,
So goodnight, folks, my rappin's all done!'

'More!' yelled the audience. 'More!'

'Curtain call?' Links asked hopefully.

But it was time to go. Oxo gave him a gentle butt and with a little bow he ran off the stage behind the others. They fled down the nearest corridor, then the one next to that, turning corners, never looking back. At last, up ahead, Wills saw the words 'Fire Exit'. As far as he was aware, they weren't on fire, but he knew what an exit was. He reared on his hind legs and banged his front hooves on the metal bar. The doors opened and the sheep tumbled out into soft, hot outdoor air at the back of the hotel.

They stood in a huddle, recovering their breath.

Behind them, in the depths of the basement, they could hear the audience – their audience – still clapping and cheering.

'Ohmygrass . . . ohmygrass . . .' burbled Jaycey, 'I'm sooo . . . sorry . . .'

They all gave her a comforting lick and tugged off her blue bow.

'Fleeced up, fleeced up, fleeced up, fleeced up . . .' gasped Sal.

'Fleeced up and ready to go,' declared Oxo.

And the reunited Warriors raised and clacked high hooves all round.

18
The Bouncing Burger
Road House

The Boombergs were twitching, trapped in the lobby, waiting for the doors to be opened. An army of cleaners was working hard, but the place was still a mess. Holly Boomberg didn't do mess. And she didn't do defeat. She kicked aside a soggy sandwich.

'Stanley,' she said sharply, 'we need a change of plan.'

'Forget the English sheep?' the Professor dared to suggest. 'Get some others?'

'No way! These ones are still perfect for the job.'

'But, honey,' Stanley tried again to show her his wrist computer. 'See this message? The team are waiting for the animals *now*. Everything else is checked and ready.'

'Let them wait,' snapped Holly. 'I will not be beaten by a bunch of ovines.' She paused for a moment, thinking. 'Anyway, *these* ones are already kitted up, remember? Do you have more sensors?'

'Well . . .'

'No, you don't. And the sensors are vital. So that's that!' She ground another sandwich to a squelching pulp beneath her foot. 'You must activate the camera.'

The Professor looked at her, startled. 'The camera?'

'Yes, dear, you know: pictures. Pictures of things. Locations. *Sheep.*'

'But it's not programmed to come on stream yet . . . it might burn out and the whole project –'

'If you don't activate it *now*, there won't be any project!'

Stanley sighed and, as he did so, the main reception lobby doors slid open. The hunt was on again.

The Warriors were trotting through downtown Las Vegas when Oxo became aware of a faint whirring in his ear. Eventually, he realised that it was something to do with the gold stud, which was suddenly warm and a bit itchy. He tried to ignore it and not make a fuss.

'Where are we going?' asked Jaycey in a subdued voice.

She was still feeling very ashamed of herself.

'Lookin' for Red Tongue, innit,' said Links, not unkindly.

Wills suddenly stopped walking. 'I think he's already gone.'

'What?' cried Oxo. 'Not again!'

Wills nodded. He was looking at a huge red neon sign which had just started flashing on a building ahead of them.

'It says, "Red Tongue does it again",' he said.

'*More* slaughtering?' asked Oxo.

'I suppose so,' said Wills.

The next lot of words flashed up and he read them aloud.

'Goodbye Las Vegas. Next stop: Aries End.'

Sal, who was a little behind the others, flopped to the pavement. Heat, exhaustion and being up so late had suddenly got the better of her.

'It's no good, dears,' she breathed, tears filling her eyes. 'You may have to go on without me . . .'

'No way,' said Oxo. 'One for all and all for –' He

looked at Sal, then froze. 'All for run!' he yelled.

The others looked up and saw what he had seen. Staple Gun Woman was creeping towards them again. Her man was carrying the rope. Oxo butted Sal to her feet and they all galloped off round the nearest corner.

'Man,' panted Links, 'that lady don't never give up . . .'

It wasn't easy for Professor Boomberg to run round corners and look at his wrist computer at the same time, especially with his wife dragging him along.

'Where are they now, dear?' she demanded. 'Where are they now?'

'Just went past a car,' puffed the Professor.

This wasn't very helpful in a town with more cars than people. Holly stopped abruptly. She grabbed her husband's wrist and peered at the computer. On its screen was a moving picture, like a tiny CCTV monitor. She saw cars and sidewalk, then the back of a sheep, then, briefly, a street sign.

'They've turned down Rhinestone Boulevard!' she cried.

The sheep were still galloping.

'We've lost them!' shouted Oxo. 'Oops. No we haven't!'

The Boombergs had appeared in front of them. The Warriors back-pedalled and skidded down an alleyway. But no matter how they zigzagged, twisted and turned, Staple Gun Woman always seemed to know where they were. And Sal was really struggling, her breaths coming in short gasps, her sides heaving even more than in the desert.

'She's runnin' on empty, man . . .' Links warned.

The Warriors were in a huge car park now, outside a tall circular building with big lights shining above it. There were rows of buses. One of them had a red trailer attached. It had double doors at the back and the doors were open. Wills dived in.

'Here! In here!' he gasped.

The other sheep jumped in behind him, Oxo and Links pushing Sal with their heads. Wills pulled the doors shut with his teeth.

'Not a sound!' he whispered in the darkness.

The Warriors stood as silently as they could with their hearts hammering. Soon they heard running footsteps. The footsteps slowed and came to a halt right outside the trailer.

Stanley leaned on the trailer for support, his legs wobbling under him. He didn't do running.

'Where have they gone?' snapped his wife.

Stanley held up his wrist to show her the blank screen.

'Cameras don't work too well in the dark,' he puffed, before she could complain.

His patience was running out as fast as his breath. There had to be easier ways to fund his projects than living with this very rich but very bossy wife. Maybe he could rob a bank or two? Holly's voice cut short his brief fantasy.

'They must have gone into the stadium. The players' tunnel is just over there. Come on . . .'

The sheep heard the humans running off. They remained motionless for a few seconds, listening intently, then began to relax. But the moment they did so, the trailer doors flew open. Something heavy whizzed over their heads and thumped on the floor. A sports bag. Then another . . . and another. The Warriors ducked and retreated.

'Ohmy–'

'Shush!' whispered Wills to Jaycey.

The storm of sports bags was followed by a shower of dirty boots and finally a football, which bounced off Oxo's head. Different human voices were approaching: loud male voices, talking excitedly.

'Any more for the trailer?' someone yelled.

No one answered the question and the trailer doors were slammed shut.

The trailer rocked a bit as the men outside got into the bus; it vibrated as the driver backed slowly out of the parking bay. Then it jolted to a halt. The Warriors heard familiar running footsteps, and a familiar voice. They held their breath again.

'Excuse me! Excuse me! Stop!'

'I already did, lady.'

The driver of the bus stared down at a smartly dressed but annoyed-looking woman clutching a length of rope. She had a ratty little man with a sweaty red face with her.

'We're looking for a flock of sheep,' said the woman breathlessly. 'Have you seen them?'

'No, lady,' replied the driver. 'I see the occasional

flying pig, but not sheep. Try Hotel English Meadows, two blocks north.' And he resumed reversing.

Holly Boomberg stepped hastily aside but, as the bus swung around and pulled away, she noticed a tuft of wool caught in the trailer doors.

'Stop!' she screamed. 'Come back! You've got our sheep!'

She raced after the departing bus and trailer. The driver saw her in his rear-view mirror and put his foot down.

'You get all kinds in Vegas . . .' he muttered.

Holly stepped in front of a passing taxi.

'Follow that bus!' she ordered as she bundled Stanley into the back seat.

The taxi driver didn't argue. You got all kinds in Vegas. Peering forward, Stanley could clearly read the words printed in black on the back of the trailer's red doors: RED TONGUE.

'Well, well,' he said, perking up. 'How about that . . .'

'How about what?' asked Holly.

'That's the team's bus,' said Stanley. '*My* team's bus. I wonder how they got on tonight.'

Holly gave him a look. She would never understand

her husband's stupid obsession with American football and Red Tongue. She leaned forward and stared at the trailer, willing it to stop.

Inside the trailer, the Warriors were being thrown from side to side.

'Sit down, guys,' yelled Wills.

They wedged themselves amongst the heap of bags and boots. One of the bags had come open and its contents had spilled out in the darkness.

'Ohmygrass . . .' said Jaycey. 'What's that smell?' She poked a pair of sweaty socks away from her nose. 'Ugh!' But it was better than the perfume of Madame Fantutti.

The bus and trailer rocked on along the highway, leaving the brilliant lights of Las Vegas far behind. The sheep wondered where they were being taken, and tried not to listen to their stomachs rumbling.

At dawn the driver pulled off the highway on to the forecourt of the Bouncing Burger Road House.

'Breakfast stop!' he yelled.

The hungry footballers piled out of the bus. Someone yanked open the trailer doors, fished around in a sports bag for some toothpaste, and then ran after the others, leaving the doors open.

The Warriors cautiously emerged from the jumble of bags.

'Let's get out and see if we can check where we are,' said Wills.

'What about Staple Gun Woman?' asked Sal.

Wills sprang from the trailer.

'We left her behind in Las Vegas,' he said.

The others jumped out too and stood stretching their legs in the car park. As they did so, a taxi turned off the highway, and for a moment, the five sheep were framed in its headlights like a photograph.

19
Tummy Trouble

The taxi slowed to a halt and Stanley Boomberg looked up from his wrist computer screen. There didn't seem to be much point in staring at it now – the sheep were there, just waiting to be captured. Holly reached for the taxi door but it was locked.

'Would you mind letting us out?' she demanded.

'Would you mind paying?' replied the driver mildly. 'Sorry to ask, lady. It's just an old-fashioned custom we taxi drivers have.'

He tapped the fare meter.

'All right, all right . . .'

Holly delved furiously in her briefcase but the taxi man didn't want any of her twenty-five credit cards.

'Sorry,' he said. 'I don't do plastic.'

Holly was becoming angry. She couldn't see the sheep any more.

'Stanley! Give the man some cash!'

'Yes, honey . . .'

But Stanley had to scrabble around in every pocket to find enough, and by the time the Boombergs had finally been released and the taxi man had gone off to breakfast with a handful of crumpled dollar bills and coins, the sheep had gone.

'Relax, honey . . .' said the Professor, feeling in charge for once. He showed Holly his wrist computer. 'I've got them. They're rootling around the trash yard.'

The Warriors had trotted around to the back of the road house. Wills was searching for a sign that would show him where they were. Everyone else was searching for food.

Oxo banged his head against one of the rubbish bins, not just because he was hungry, but also because the gold stud in his ear was beginning to drive him mad with its pinching.

'Ohmygrass, you're making it bleed,' cried Jaycey, but Oxo went on banging.

A waitress, who'd seen them from the kitchen doorway, suddenly strode over.

'Is that thing bothering you?' she asked, taking hold

of Oxo's ear and peering at the gold stud. 'Who would do this to a dumb animal?'

She prised open the staple with her kitchen scissors and removed the stud from Oxo's ear.

'Is that better?' she asked, holding it in the palm of her hand for Oxo to see.

Oxo put his nose into her hand and snaffled up the stud. He chewed once or twice, then swallowed. The waitress laughed and went back to the kitchen.

'Why in Ovis did you do that?' asked Wills.

Oxo shrugged defensively. 'Habit, I suppose. Well, when humans hold a hand out, there's usually something in it to eat, isn't there?' He waggled his ear. 'Anyway, feels great now. Which way do we go?'

'Uh . . . that way,' said Wills.

He nodded to a narrow stony road, a hikers' trail, leading from the back of the service area into the desert hills. A small wooden signpost stood beside it.

'That says "Short Cut to Aries End",' he said.

'What's a short cut?' asked Oxo suspiciously.

He'd heard about cuts of meat. He didn't fancy being a short cut. Not even a long cut.

'It's just a quick way to get somewhere,' said Wills.

'I expect the highway goes there too but takes longer.'

'And remind me why Aries End is important?' said Sal.

'It's where Red Tongue's goin' next, innit,' said Links excitedly.

'Yeah,' said Oxo. 'It's where we're gonna have the final showdown. So let's not keep him waiting.'

And he led the gallop on to the narrow, winding road.

The Boombergs had stopped on the other side of the bins while the Professor stared at his wrist, suddenly bemused.

'Lost the picture again,' he muttered.

'We don't *need* the picture any more, Stanley. They're there, behind the bins!'

But they weren't. When Holly crept quietly around, noose at the ready, she met with nothing but the grey dawn of the desert.

'This is awesome . . .' The Professor was still staring at his wrist screen. 'They're in some weird wobbly cave full of sloshy stuff!'

Inspiration struck his wife.

'The bins!' she cried. 'They must be in these bins! Help me tip them over!'

They tried the organic waste first. They manhandled the head-high bin against a kerb and toppled it on its side.

'Hey!' shouted the waitress from the kitchen. 'What are you doing?'

Making a horrible mess for nothing was what they were doing, and ruining Holly's smart shoes while they were doing it. The bin was indeed full of sloshy stuff. It rolled and gushed all over the tarmac, and up Professor Boomberg's legs. But there were no sheep amid the half-eaten burgers and yesterday's ice cream.

As the waitress strode from the kitchen again, Holly heard an engine start. She spun around. Inspiration had struck again.

'The trailer! Of course! They're back in the trailer!'

She raced after the departing bus, caught hold of the trailer doors and yanked them open. As she threw herself inside, she turned and grabbed her husband's outstretched arm, and hauled him in after her. The Professor landed flat on his face and the trailer turned on to the highway with his legs still sticking out of the open doors. Holly was already rummaging amongst the sports bags.

'They're here somewhere . . .' she muttered. 'I can *smell* them.'

The Professor could smell all kinds of things, mostly on his trousers. He wobbled to his feet and banged his head on the roof of the trailer.

'They *were* here, honey,' he said through gritted teeth. 'Were . . .' And he gazed at his wrist in wonder. The picture on the screen now looked like the inside of an active volcano.

The bus had picked up speed and was cruising along the highway with the players inside singing:

'We're on our way to Aries End, Red Tongue, Red Tongue! On our way to Aries End, Red Tongue, remember the name!'

Gradually, the players became aware of thumps and shouts from the trailer behind them. The driver pulled over to the side of the highway and they all got out to investigate.

'We were merely looking for our sheep,' said Holly primly, as she slid out and pulled Stanley after her.

'What's with you and sheep, lady?' demanded the driver.

'They were here! Can't you smell them?' demanded Holly.

The players sniffed.

'That's Dave's socks!' one of them laughed, slamming the trailer doors.

Stanley just had time to ask some of the players for their autographs before the driver ushered them back into the bus.

'I'm a great fan,' the Professor whispered, taking back his pocket-sized copy of *Physics For Unbelievably Brainy People*.

'Stanley!'

His wife was already striding back along the highway towards the Bouncing Burger. The Professor loped guiltily after her.

The Warriors were marching on towards Aries End. After the bumpy darkness of the trailer, they actually enjoyed the early sun's warmth on their backs. Except for Oxo.

Oxo did not feel good. It was rare for him to regret

eating anything, but ever since he'd swallowed the gold stud, every one of his stomachs had been churning. Eventually, he stumbled and sat on the dirt road, his sides quivering.

'Are you all right, dear?' asked Sal.

'Course I am,' said Oxo.

He struggled to his hooves and staggered on, but a few minutes later he was sitting again.

'Better stop, innit,' said Links. 'There's a bit of shade up there . . .'

The small patch of shade was cast by a battered truck parked a little way ahead of them. Two men in dusty clothes and boots were digging in the desert close by. They hadn't noticed the sheep.

'We're wasting our time, Gramps,' the younger man said, stopping to wipe the sweat from his face. 'There ain't no gold here.'

The older man kept on digging. 'Sure is *somewhere*, Brad . . .' he said. 'Jumpy Joe's map's clear enough. Give or take a mile . . .'

'But if Jumpy Joe never found it a hundred years ago, how we gonna find it now?'

'By *believin'*, boy,' puffed Gramps. 'You gotta

have faith. And dig. Go get the map again.'

Brad dropped his shovel, turned towards the truck, and stopped.

'Hey, Gramps . . .' he said in amazement. 'Looks like lunch just arrived.'

Both men stared at the little group of sheep.

'Well blow me to San Francisco . . .' laughed Gramps. 'Where did you all come from?' Then he stopped smiling. 'One of the poor critters looks sick,' he said.

The biggest of the sheep was staggering badly. It just reached the shade of the truck before it keeled over and collapsed.

20
Gold Fever

As Oxo lay panting in the shade, he knew he was going to be sick.

'Scuse me . . .' he mumbled and dragged himself to the other side of the track.

The gold stud came up in a sticky, smelly mess of half-chewed plastic grass.

'Here, fella, have a drink . . .'

Oxo suddenly found an old man squatting beside him. He'd poured some water into his upturned hat and was holding it out. A younger man was standing close by. Oxo gratefully slurped a few mouthfuls then tottered back to the other sheep.

'Sorry about that,' he said. 'All gone.'

The young man was still standing by the pile of sick. He slowly bent forward to peer at the recent contents of Oxo's stomach. Something had caught his eye.

'Gramps . . .' he said, his voice little more than a whisper. 'Look at this.' He crouched and picked the gold stud from the soggy pile. 'Gold . . . a nugget of gold!'

He wiped the lump of chewed metal on his sleeve and held it up. Gramps stared, and then snatched the stud, put it between his front teeth and bit it.

'Well?' asked Brad anxiously.

Gramps cackled and creaked to his feet, waving the stud.

'It's gold, sure enough!' he cried. 'A hungry ole ram's found Jumpy Joe's gold! What did I tell you, boy?' He grabbed his shovel and began digging manically at the road. 'Tell Uncle Silas,' he said. 'But no one else. This is *our* find, boy! Ours!'

Brad ran across to the campfire smouldering beside their truck. He held his hat over the flames for a moment, then moved it aside. A puff of white smoke rose into the still desert air. He did it again and another puff of smoke rose. When he'd finished sending his message, he spat on his hands, seized a pickaxe and attacked the road beside Gramps.

The Warriors had been watching with interest.

'Sometimes,' said Oxo, 'it's very hard to understand humans.'

'Are you all right to go on now, dear?' asked Sal.

'I'm right as rain now I've got rid of that,' said Oxo.

'Oh wouldn't that be nice,' sighed Jaycey. 'Some rain!'

They each took a quick sip of water from Gramps' upturned hat, then trotted away.

The Boombergs had hoped to hire a truck when they got back to the Bouncing Burger, but there was none to be had so they were forced to make do with a motorbike. While it was being filled with fuel, Holly looked around for clues.

'That's the way they went,' she said, pointing at hoofprints on the track behind the rubbish bins.

Apart from saying 'Short Cut', the sign to Aries End said 'No Trucks, No Autos, No Bikes' but Holly Boomberg didn't *do* no. She sped away into the arid hills, doing a wheelie, with Stanley clinging on behind.

Peering ahead, Holly could see puffs of white smoke in the distance. It soon became obvious that she wasn't the only one who ignored road signs. A four-by-four swept past the motorbike in a cloud of fumes and dust. Then another . . . and another. All kinds of vehicles, motor and horse-drawn, appeared from nowhere, jostling for position on the narrow track.

Gramps and Brad stopped digging and gazed at the fast-approaching swarm of uninvited fortune hunters.

'I'm always tellin' you we should get ourselves a cell phone, Gramps,' said Brad.

'Maybe you're right, son,' agreed Gramps. 'Smoke signals ain't that private nowadays.'

He fumbled for a match, then lit a fuse and stuck his fingers in his ears. The explosion that followed was a tad bigger than he'd anticipated; he was a bit rusty when it came to dynamite. It blew out a huge crater of sand and rock, which, though it didn't reveal any gold, did entirely block the track.

As the greedy army of vehicles began arriving, a couple on a motorbike skidded to a halt in front of Gramps and Brad.

'Clear the road!' shouted the woman, glaring at the mountain of impassable rubble behind Gramps. 'We have to get through!'

Gramps shrugged. 'Not today you ain't, lady, leastways, not on that.' He eyed the motorbike. Brad had always wanted one. 'But I'll swap you my mule for that there thing.'

Holly quickly made up her mind.

'Come on, Stanley,' she snapped, and scrambled off the bike.

'Mind she don't bite now,' Gramps called after her, but not loud enough for Holly to hear.

Tod and Gran had been locked up for one whole day and a night, which was long enough for them to have excavated a tunnel under the jail house wall. Tod had done the digging while Gran carried away the dirt in her hat and found places to hide it. The sun had just come up on the second day of their imprisonment and they were getting excited.

'We're nearly there,' said Tod, wriggling backwards out of the tunnel and handing another shovel-load of dirt to Gran. 'I can see daylight – it must be from the street.'

Gran had filled the little stove and both bunk beds, and was just starting to top up her handbag with Tod's latest load when they heard Sheriff Tiny arriving in the outer office.

The prisoners scurried to their beds, jumped in on top of their piles of dirt and stones, and pulled the blankets up to their chins. The overloaded mattresses sagged and groaned beneath them. Sheriff Tiny was whistling and carrying a breakfast tray.

'I hope you slept well, ma'am?' he said courteously.

'Like a rock,' replied Gran.

'A pile of rocks,' confirmed Tod.

'I have to do my rounds,' said Tiny, sliding the tray beneath the bars into the cell. 'When I come back, we'll have a proper chat about your friend Mr Rhubarb.' He gave Gran a stern look. 'Maybe you'll have seen sense by then.'

'And maybe you'll have seen our sheep,' she replied.

When the sheriff had gone, Tod and Gran devoured the breakfast. After all the hard work, they were starving.

'I've never thought of putting syrup on my bacon,' said Gran as they munched. 'Lovely. One to try when we get back home. Maybe with a couple of chillies.'

Tod just nodded. Home seemed an awfully long way away.

They'd just started digging again when the new day's first group of tourists wandered into the sheriff's office.

'Great show,' said one of them.

'Glad you're enjoying it,' replied Gran, thrusting a hatful of stony dirt through the bars. 'Get rid of that, would you?'

Back in gold-fever country, the Warriors had heard the dynamite explosion behind them but they had more urgent things to worry about. Wills was afraid they might be going the wrong way. There were no more signs to Aries End, and the track they were following had become narrower and was descending sharply now, with the steep red hills on either side becoming cliffs, hemming the sheep in. If anything ahead blocked their way, there would scarcely be room to turn round. They would be trapped.

And then Jaycey, who was in front for once, suddenly stopped.

'Ohmygrass . . .' she whimpered. 'He's here. We've foundhimfoundhimfoundhim . . .'

The other Warriors crowded as close as they could to see. There, on the sandy track before them, was the biggest claw print they had ever had nightmares about.

21
The Devil's Stovepipe

'Why've you stopped?' cried Holly, kicking the mule.

It didn't respond. It just stood where it was, quivering with fear. The Boombergs were at the top of the steeply descending track behind the sheep, and Holly could see them some way below.

'They're just *standing* there,' she said, twisting around to talk to Stanley, who was riding pillion just as he'd done on the motorbike.

'Maybe there's something stopping them going on any further,' said the Professor, peering over his wife's shoulder.

There was. And not only the claw print. The track in front of the Warriors widened out slightly into a tiny clearing, which was littered with boulders and branches, ripped from the hills above by the recent sandstorm. Filling the narrow clearing between the cliffs, standing on its hind legs like a human, poised ready to attack, was a monster. It had black fur, black eyes, bared yellow teeth . . . and a red tongue.

Jaycey was speechless. She wanted to squeal her loudest-ever squeal but she couldn't. Her voice, like the rest of her, was melting into a jelly of fear.

The great beast raised its head and roared. It lashed out, its claws slicing the air, and the Warriors jumped back. To Wills' amazement, the beast didn't follow. It just stood there, swaying and roaring and slashing the air in frustrated anger. And pain.

Wills was trying to remember the pictures he'd seen in Tod's school books.

'I think it's a bear,' he said.

'IsthatbetterthanRedTongue?' blabbered Jaycey. 'Dobearseatsheep?'

'Man, it's big enough to eat a horse,' gulped Links.

The bear roared again, and this time they all heard the pain.

'What's the matter with it?' asked Oxo. 'Why doesn't it come for us?'

'Stuck, innit.' Links nodded and for the first time

the other sheep noticed the fallen tree trunk lying in front of the bear. The animal's hind paws were trapped beneath it.

'Well that's all right then,' said Oxo briskly. 'Onwards?'

'We can't just leave it!' cried Sal. 'It'll die of hunger!'

'Oh,' said Oxo, for whom dying of hunger was the worst fate imaginable. 'Right.'

'But it could kill us all, man,' pointed out Links. 'And we ain't never gonna find the Red Tongue dude if we's dead.'

'Nevertheless,' said Sal, taking a deep breath, 'it is a fellow creature. Jaycey, stay here and do something.'

'*Do* something?' squeaked Jaycey.

'Yes, dear, distract it. While the rest of us move that log.'

With her body pressed against the cliff, Sal began to edge past the bear. The others followed. The beast snarled and growled and twisted from side to side, and they all felt the rush of air as its fearsome claws swept past their heads.

'Ohmygrassohmygrass . . .' Jaycey tried to be distracting. She tossed her pretty head and examined her front hooves. 'Um . . . how d'you keep your claws sharp?' she enquired.

The others lined themselves up behind the bear, which had now turned away from them and was growling suspiciously at Jaycey.

'Ready!' cried Sal. 'Charge!'

Oxo was a bit cross that she'd used his word but this was no time for petty jealousies. The Warriors lowered their heads and charged the fallen log. The bear swivelled its head to see what they were doing and lashed sideways with a paw.

'Again!' shouted Oxo before Sal could speak.

The sheep ignored the huge teeth and the hot breath on their shoulders and rammed the log a second time. It rocked and rolled, but with their heads down, they didn't see the bear writhing free.

'One more . . .' shouted Oxo. 'A longer run-up this time.'

Jaycey was still bravely bobbing about and chattering about keeping claws and hooves in trim when the huge creature lurched towards her.

'Ohmygrass!' she screamed. And then, 'Ohmygrass . . .' again, as the ground behind the bear seemed to open up and swallow her fellow Warriors.

They'd done as Oxo instructed and backed away a little further to get a longer run-up at the log. And since they were moving backwards, they hadn't seen the huge hole behind them.

'Ohmygrassgrassgrass . . .' whimpered Jaycey.

She'd heard her friends' cries as they disappeared. Now she could only hear the snuffling, grunting noise as the bear leaned forward and closed its huge jaws around her neck.

Jaycey became speechless again. Frozen. But there was no bite. No pain at all. Jaycey felt herself being lifted off the ground and carried very gently in the bear's mouth. Then she was looking down into a deep, dark nothingness. The bear opened its jaws and Jaycey's hooves scampered in thin air.

From their seat on the mule, the Boombergs had watched the sheep's rescue of the bear in open-mouthed wonder. Stanley was impressed and alarmed in equal measure.

'Honey, maybe these creatures are *really really* too clever? I mean, we wouldn't want them kind of taking over the project. Messing up the experiments or anything.'

His wife was sitting bolt upright, only half listening, her mind racing.

'I don't think we need worry about *that*, dear,' she said. 'Don't you see where we are?'

Stanley gazed vaguely around. He hated questions he couldn't answer.

'Arizona's where we are, dear,' he said.

'We're at the top of the Devil's Stovepipe,' declared Holly, turning to him.

Stanley looked blank.

'Close to home!' continued his wife. 'It's a natural air vent. It goes all the way down to our place. I can't remember quite where the bottom is, but that hole is quite definitely the top.'

'Uh-huh,' said Stanley, but he was no longer listening.

He was watching the bear. Since dropping the sheep down the hole, it had been squatting at the edge, looking down and making weird little noises. Stanley fancied it was saying thank you, which was ridiculous and unscientific. But now it had straightened up and turned to face *him*. The Professor instantly forgot that today was B-Day.

Holly wasn't looking at the bear. Stanley obviously hadn't grasped the true significance of what he'd just witnessed.

'A natural air vent, Stanley . . .' she repeated. 'A fissure in the rock? A hole that drops down a very, very long way?'

There was still no response from her husband, who was staring over her shoulder, his face chalky white.

'I'm afraid your sheep are now a heap of very broken bones at the rocky foot of the Stovepipe,' said Holly. 'Really really clever, but history.'

But if Holly still wasn't aware of the now advancing bear, both Stanley and the mule certainly were. The mule suddenly whinnied in terror, wheeled round and galloped off, while Holly grappled with the reins and Stanley hung on for dear life.

'But don't worry,' yelled Holly. 'Your entire life's ambition is not down the tubes!'

Stanley's fingers dug deeper into Holly's sides as he felt himself slipping backwards.

A whimpering, 'It's not?' was all he could manage in reply.

His wife turned to him. Her eyes were sparkling, despite the bumpy ride as the mule careered off the track.

'Not one bit of it,' she shouted. 'We must replace the sheep, that's all. How about a couple of humans instead? Two very disposable humans!'

22
High Noon

Sheriff Tiny had never known a morning like it. Suddenly, he'd been required to do real sheriffing all over the place.

Only ten minutes ago, he'd met up with a hungry bear and frightened it off with his shotgun, which he hadn't had an excuse to fire in years. Then he'd come across a bitey varmint of a stray mule and bravely captured that. So what with bears and mules and gold rushes and illegal explosions, he'd forgotten all about the little old lady and the boy and their sob story about lost sheep and rhubarb. And now, to cap it all, a couple of strangers had appeared, hurrying out of a side track towards him: a thin, sweaty little man wearing filthy trousers; and a strong-looking woman, wearing high-heeled shoes and carrying a briefcase.

On seeing Tiny, the woman waved vigorously.

'Yoohoo . . .' she called pleasantly, as if she were on an afternoon stroll in the park.

As the sheriff reined in Lightning and the mule and waited for the strangers, Holly nudged Stanley.

'Be careful what you say,' she warned. 'He's wearing a badge. Don't mention Back of Beyond Ranch.'

Stanley had no intention of mentioning anything at all. He rubbed his bruised bottom and stared miserably at his wrist computer.

'They've switched to final countdown mode,' he muttered.

'Howdy,' said the sheriff. 'This mule belong to you folks, by any chance?'

'It does indeed,' cried Holly gaily. 'It got spooked by a bear and threw us off.'

Stanley winced at the recent memory.

'Thank you so much for finding it,' continued Holly.

She took the mule's reins from the sheriff, jumped on and helped Stanley up. In front of her this time, as he was always falling off at the back. With a little wave, she turned the mule and headed back along the main trail. Sheriff Tiny ignored the wave and trotted alongside.

'Nice day for a gold rush,' he remarked cheerfully as they rode. 'Did you see the mess they made back here?'

Holly nodded.

Tiny chuckled. 'Just like the old times . . .' he said. 'You folks touring?'

Holly nodded again.

'Where you headin' next?'

'Back of B–'

'Back to civilisation,' cut in Holly, giving Stanley a shut-up kick.

'Oh,' said Tiny, pleased. 'Gunslinger City? Me too. Not that *I'm* on vacation like you folks, mind. Nosirree . . . Got a coupla prisoners to interrogate. Bein' a sheriff and all.' The thrill of suddenly being important was loosening his tongue. 'Coupla non-residents I picked up at Back of Beyond Ranch.' He shook his head and chuckled again. 'Claim to have lost a bunch of rare sheep and be friends of "Mr Rhubarb".'

The Professor almost fell off the mule, despite being at the front. Holly stopped him, her fist clenched tightly on his collar.

'How very interesting,' she managed to say. 'We'd love to visit Gunslinger, wouldn't we, dear?'

A while later, in Gunslinger City itself, Tod's head popped up in the main street. He'd pushed out the last few inches of dirt like a mole hill. The tunnel from inside the cell was complete.

The sun blinded him and it was several seconds before he could see that the street was pretty much deserted: most tourists were in the café, keeping out of the midday heat. Tod scrabbled backwards under the cell wall and rejoined Gran inside.

'Coast's clear, Gran,' he said eagerly. 'You go first, then I can give you a push if you need one.'

Gran didn't need a push. It was hard on her old bones but she wriggled through the tunnel.

'We're free!' she exclaimed as Tod joined her outside.

They stood for a moment, blinking in the sunlight, not quite sure what to do next. And unaware that the decision was about to be taken away from them.

*

Holly Boomberg had no idea what they were going to do when they reached Gunslinger City. Breaking a couple of prisoners out of jail was going to be difficult, but it had to be done. B-Day had arrived. And as the sheep were dead, they had to get their hands on the human substitutes. She would not be beaten.

They were just entering the main street when the sheriff brought Lightning to an abrupt halt. Holly looked up and saw why. The old woman and the boy were standing there, talking earnestly outside the jail house.

'Well, I'll be hornswoggled . . .'

Sheriff Tiny leaped from his horse, intending to creep up on the escaped prisoners. But when Tod and Gran saw him, they didn't run away. Quite the opposite.

'That's them!' Tod was pointing as the sheriff strode towards him. 'The people who kidnapped us!'

'That's Rhubarb!' shouted Gran.

Then they were both charging past the sheriff, towards the couple on the mule.

'What have you done with our flock?' they both yelled together.

'I don't know what you're talking about,' blustered Holly, looking down at the boy who was tearing towards her. 'We've never seen you before in our lives, have we, dear?'

Stanley didn't have time to answer.

'Oh yes you have!' Tod turned briefly back to the sheriff. 'He's got a wrist computer! A very clever one. Come and see!'

Holly took one last look at Tod's angry face, then one long look at the sheriff's frown, and knew for certain that the game was up. The man with the badge on his chest was going to be asking some very awkward questions. She slid from the mule, dragging Stanley with her.

The boy was right in front of her now and the sheriff was coming back too, breaking into a run. Holly looked around and grabbed the reins dangling from Lightning's back.

'Get on!' she screamed at Stanley.

She slipped her foot into the stirrup and leapt on to the great horse's back before leaning down, grabbing Stanley's outstretched arms and dragging him on behind her.

'Go! Go! Go!' she shrieked, slapping the reins and kicking her heels.

Lightning took off like a rocket.

23
Fool's Gold Canyon

Tourists were squeezing out of the café to see what new show was being performed in the street. They applauded as the couple on a large white horse galloped away, leaving the sheriff standing, wheezing for breath. The boy was nodding his head vigorously as the ancient lady at his side spoke to him. Suddenly, he turned and ran towards the tourists. A patient pony, harnessed to a trap, a small two-wheeled tourist carriage, was tethered outside the café. The boy untied it and helped the ancient lady on to the driver's seat.

'Hup! Hup!' she cried, slapping the reins.

The boy leapt on beside her.

'Hup! Hup!'

The pony responded and trotted away. The old lady whooped louder and the pony broke into a canter. The chase was on. The tourists cheered. Sheriff Tiny was left standing with the bitey mule.

'Faster, you galumphing great brute!' yelled Holly at Lightning, whose name, after his initial burst, was proving a bit of an exaggeration. She glanced over her shoulder, past her husband's scared face, towards the pursuing pony and trap. 'Don't worry, darling,' she shouted.

'Of course I'm worried,' yelled back Stanley. 'Today's B-Day! My only chance for success and fame and adulation and –'

'I know, dear,' yelled Holly. 'And all will be well!'

The Professor held on tight. He had to hand it to his wife: pessimism was not her middle name.

There were bats in the barn at Eppingham Farm and, when not composing raps, Links had sometimes wondered what it must be like to sleep upside down. Not that he was sleeping now; but he *was* experiencing that hanging upside down thing. Several of the sheep were, and had been for some time.

Having tumbled down the deep hole that was the Devil's Stovepipe, they'd been saved from becoming a pile of broken bones by a pile of broken branches. A matted tangle of dead foliage and fallen boughs had collected halfway down the narrow chasm, like a giant fur ball. And although it had creaked and snapped and slipped as, one by one, the Warriors landed on it, the tangle hadn't given way completely, not even when Jaycey landed on top of the pile, dropped by the bear.

So there they were, snagged and dangling. Links began to wriggle and rap.

'This bein' a bat is only so-so,
We's hangin' doin' nothun
When we should be go-go.
We gotta finish Red Tongue,
At ole Aries End,
So we is outta here, man,
This forest gotta bend ~'

The rap became a snap, then a crack, as Links struggled to dislodge himself.

'Whooaa . . . easy, twiggy tingies!' he cried, as the twisted mass around him began to slip.

'OhmyshutupLinks!' squealed Jaycey. 'We're slippingslippingslipping!'

'Tuck your legs in, guys!' called Wills. 'So they don't break when we hit the bottom . . .'

There was a rapid scraping of sticks against the rock wall, a lot of dry rustling and shrill bleating, then a heavy thump. And silence.

Links sat up. In the dim light at the bottom of the rock chimney, he counted four other sheep, which was good. And they were all on top of the woody, leafy, rafty thingy like he was, which was even better.

'Hey . . .' he said, nodding. 'Cool ride, eh, man?'

'And not a broken leg between us,' pointed out Sal, struggling upright.

'Yeah, thanks a bunch, Links,' said Oxo, though he sounded a bit sarcastic. 'But there's still nothing to eat.'

The Warriors squeezed out of the Stovepipe through a feeble strip of wire mesh, and found themselves in a cool, cave-like passageway, dimly illuminated by lights in the ceiling. There was no sign to Aries End but there was no way back either: they could never climb the Stovepipe.

Wills didn't know much about the inside of

mountains, but the wire mesh and the lights were a surprise. He tried to sound positive.

'This way,' he called.

Everyone followed him as he marched off down the winding, rocky passage.

On the far side of the hill into which the sheep had fallen, Gran and Tod were beginning to gain on Lightning and the Rhubarbs.

They'd left the track from Gunslinger City now, and the ground was becoming rougher and steeper as the hills closed in around them. The four humans were alone. Holly turned her head and yelled at her husband.

'Open your eyes, Stanley! We're nearly there. Contact control. Tell them to open the doors.'

It wasn't easy for Stanley to dab instructions into his wrist computer whilst clinging to his wife's back, but he managed.

'Done . . .' he called, hoping she wouldn't demand anything else of him.

'Good.'

Holly turned to him again and to the Professor's astonishment she began to grin widely.

'They're all yours, darling,' she purred. 'Flies buzzing into a web . . .'

Stanley didn't have a clue what his wife was talking about. He risked a peep ahead, over her shoulder, and a surge of relief flooded through him. Right in front of them a steel door, painted the dull-red colour of the desert, was opening in the side of the hill.

An amazed Tod and Gran also saw the square gap appear. They saw Lightning gallop through, taking the Rhubarbs with him.

'What should we do, Gran?' yelled Tod, bracing himself for impact, expecting the doors to slam shut.

Gran slapped the reins and urged her pony on. 'Too late to stop!' she shouted.

The pony and trap rattled through the doorway after Lightning and skewed to a halt. Tod leapt to the ground, ready to face whatever might be in front of him. He was aware of a massive concrete floor, a rocky cavern and dim artificial light. Then a voice.

'Excellent, my dears. Welcome to Fool's Gold Canyon!'

24
The Countdown

'There you are, darling,' said Holly Boomberg to her husband. 'My plan worked. They've ridden right into my trap.'

Stanley didn't believe her for a minute. *He* was the clever one. His wife was just lucky. And rich, of course, which was the same thing. He didn't *want* humans. But he had no choice now. He turned to a quickly arriving group of men and women in white coats.

'Get the boy and the old woman weighed and measured straight away,' he barked. 'And recalculate the loads.'

'You're going to use humans?' said one of the women, her eyes wide in disbelief.

'Don't ask questions, just do it,' snapped the Professor. 'My wife failed to get the sheep I wanted.'

Holly felt deeply hurt, but bit her lip and tried not

to show it. Her husband, she reminded herself, was a genius on the brink of his most daring experiment. The moment had come to set light to all the money she'd piled on him and his cleverness. He was bound to be feeling tense and snappy just now. Success and fame were just minutes away. For both of them.

Tod found himself being pulled to his feet by the people in white coats. More of them had hold of his gran.

'What's going on?' he shouted.

'You are,' replied Holly, regaining her composure. 'You're going on a journey.' She nodded at one of the white coats. 'Look after the nags,' she ordered.

She led the way into the vast man-made cavern, followed by her husband and Tod and Ida, who were being frog-marched along by two white coats each. Several white coats hurried in front and even more came behind. Holly suddenly stopped and nodded and smiled at her husband.

'This is Professor Stanley Boomberg, by the way,' she said. 'Creator of this secret place. And it's him you have to thank.'

'For what?' said Tod.

'The chance to be part of Boom Day.'

Stanley smiled, then glanced at his wrist computer. Holly took the hint and marched on, finally reaching a set of double doors marked PREPARATION ROOM. The doors swung open automatically and the Boombergs marched through. The white coats pushed their prisoners in behind.

Tod quickly scanned his new surroundings. They were in a small room with glass walls. Through the glass walls he could see an enormous, dimly lit space, where banks of computers were manned by more white coats with tense expressions. The digital wall clocks were clicking, and he could hear an automated voice speaking the countdown aloud.

In the very middle of the space, beyond the computers, stood a cone-shaped structure, about the size of Gran's garden shed, draped in a white cloth. Looking up, Tod saw that the roof of the cavern above was perfectly domed. And there was something else very odd about the roof: it was cracked in a straight line down the centre, and the crack was slowly widening. The roof was rolling back, allowing a thin shaft of daylight to cut through.

'Take a seat,' said the Professor, giving Tod a little shove.

Tod turned his attention back to the room. In the middle were two padded chairs, like those at the dentist's. They were fixed side by side and surrounded by machines with wires.

'Just a few checks and tests before we install you,' continued the Professor. 'We have to rebalance everything because you're not sheep.'

'Where *are* our sheep?' asked Gran, struggling as a couple of white coats pushed her roughly into one of the chairs.

The Professor shrugged. 'Wherever dead sheep go, I guess.'

'Dead?' Gran stopped struggling. '*Dead?*'

She was already looking frail and tired after her heroic drive. Now she collapsed into the chair. Tod's anger boiled over. He writhed and kicked and it took the combined strength of both Boombergs plus several white coats to snap a seat harness across his chest, pinning him to the other chair.

'What's all this about?' he demanded. 'What are you up to?'

'My husband,' answered Holly, straightening up and looking down at Tod, 'has invented a new type of rocket. It can go further and faster than any rocket ever before.'

Stanley nodded with more modesty than he felt.

'*And*,' continued his wife, 'he has also discovered a new planet.' She beamed with pride. 'He's named it Petunia. Because that's my middle name.'

The white coat standing nearest to Tod raised her eyebrows.

'Should be Bossyboots really,' she muttered under her breath.

'I calculate that this new planet's a lot like Earth,' said the Professor, ignoring the white coat. 'Florida, actually. But before I can be sure, I need to conduct some survival experiments. Using live species, of course.'

'That was why we wanted your sheep,' added Holly. 'The Professor has devised a number of data-gathering tasks, which the creatures he sends must complete before they're allowed food. He needs animals that are bright but not too bright.'

Stanley was nodding in agreement as he checked dials on the machines. His wife was managing to explain his amazingly complex work in quite simple terms. He almost liked her for a moment.

'It's a pity about your sheep,' he said with a shrug. 'The instruments we attached to their ears were highly advanced. They'd have transmitted some very useful information and pictures.'

'Never mind, darling.' Holly was almost jigging up and down with excitement. Stanley had never seen her so . . . unHolly-like. 'The world is about to be amazed,' she declared. 'Professor Stanley Boomberg, *my* husband, will be hailed as the greatest egghead in the universe!'

'Egghead, dear?' questioned the Professor, with a pained smile.

'Sorry, darling. Scientific genius.'

'You're mad,' gasped Tod.

'Nothing wrong with being mad,' said Stanley. 'So long as you're right.'

'*Lots* of people have called my husband mad,' said Holly, doing a little twirl. 'All the scientists he's ever worked with called him mad. But they're merely jealous, because they haven't discovered the new Florida. Tomorrow he will be famous. *I* will be famous. The name Boomberg will be famous.' She held a finger poised over a button on the arm of Tod's chair. 'May I?' she asked.

The Professor nodded indulgently. Holly pressed the button. The glass wall between the smaller room and the main chamber slid open, and both chairs began to move. The people in white coats looked up from their screens and clapped as the chairs carried Gran and Tod smoothly towards the covered cone shape beyond the computers.

'You can't send my gran into space!' yelled Tod.

Holly was walking proudly beside his moving chair and he grabbed her arm fiercely.

'Send me, but let Gran go! She's too old.'

'She might enjoy Petunia,' cooed Holly. 'Lots of people retire to Florida. And you'd better get used to it too.' She shook her arm free and gave Tod's hand a little pinch. 'Did we forget to tell you? The rocket can only carry enough fuel to get there. It will never come back.'

The chairs came to a halt. Peering down, Tod saw that they had reached the edge of a deep shaft. He could now see that the cone shape wasn't actually sitting *on* the cavern floor at all. It was joined to a tubular body that descended into the shaft. Its base was somewhere far below. What he was facing was just the tip of the tube: the nose cone of a huge space rocket. Short metal walkways bridged the gap between the cavern floor and the cloth-draped cone.

Tod gulped and looked upwards. The dome-shaped roof of the cavern had completely rolled back now, and he could see a perfect circle of blue sky directly above the rocket.

Stanley smiled over Tod's head at his wife.

'Tell the guys to skip a few thousand from the countdown, dear,' he said. 'Let's breathe some fire.'

'Let's breathe some fire!' shouted Holly into a nearby microphone. 'Let's Boom!'

25
Oxo's Last Charge

The Warriors had been trotting in single file through rocky tunnels for what seemed like hours. They were all nervous underground and wishing they could see the burning sun instead of the dim ceiling lights.

Wills hoped against hope that they wouldn't round a narrow corner and come face to face with Red Tongue. They would have to do battle with him one by one, and he didn't fancy their chances in that situation.

'Ohmygrass,' whispered Jaycey. 'I can hear something . . .'

They stopped to listen. Somewhere ahead of them a voice, not quite human, was intoning numbers:

'Two hundred and ninety-nine . . . Two hundred and ninety-eight . . . Two hundred and ninety-seven . . .'

Sal gulped in horror. 'Is that *it* counting?' she asked. 'As it eats the poor sheep it's captured?'

They peered into the dimness of the tunnel. A hot, burning smell now filled their nostrils and someone or some*thing* was roaring.

'Ohmygrass . . . ohmygrass,' whimpered Jaycey. 'Have we got to go on?'

'Sure smells like the breath of the Red Tongue dude . . .' muttered Links.

Then there was another sound.

'Grannnnnn!' Tod's anguished wail echoed along the tunnel.

'That sounded human, innit,' said Links, his eyes wide and scared.

'It *sounded* like Tod,' said Wills. 'But it couldn't be. He's safe back home in Eppingham.' He shook his head, trying to think clearly. 'Well, Sal . . . *do* we go on?'

'Are we Warriors?' Sal cried.

She squeezed past the others to the front and marched on down the tunnel. Links brought up the rear. He was just as frightened as the rest, but his voice rang out boldly.

'Red Tongue, you said to remember your name,
Now the time has come to finish your game.

We was called out here by the Songs of the Fleece,

And until you's gone we won't get no peace . . .'

Not far from the marching Warriors, in the huge cavern now open to the sky, Tod and Gran could do nothing but stare at the little ceremony that was taking place. Tod was silent now after his shout of despair. The Professor, with an excited gleam in his eye, was about to cut the cord holding the white cloth over the rocket's nose.

'Ready?' he asked. 'It's going to be a big surprise.'

Holly nodded. She rather hoped her husband had painted her face on the rocket's nose cone. How wonderful that would be. Holly Petunia Boomberg, immortalised as her image sped heavenwards.

'I'm ready, dear,' she said.

The Professor cut the cord and the cloth was whisked away. Holly had to bite her lip again to hide her disappointment. Bite it very hard. Stanley didn't notice.

'Isn't it fantastic?' he said, above the polite applause from the watching white coats.

The rocket had been painted to look like a fierce

dog's head, with bloodshot eyes, drawn-back ears and a black nose. The jaws, which were wide open, formed a doorway into the rocket. Looking into the darkness beyond the doorway was like looking into the mouth of a gigantic hound. Two rows of sharp white teeth had been painted inside the doorway, one at the top and one at the bottom, and beneath it lolled a huge painted red tongue.

'I'm a great football fan,' explained the Professor, leaning down to talk to Tod. 'The Prairie Dogs, you know? I thought it would be kind of nice for Red Tongue to be way up there, looking down on the Rams.' He checked his wrist computer. 'This is it,' he said, stepping back from the chairs. 'Come on, honey, stand away now.'

The chairs, with Tod and Ida strapped in place, slid across the bridge over the deep shaft, and through the narrow door into the nose cone.

At that moment, the Warriors emerged from the end of their long, winding tunnel. They stood blinking in the sudden daylight. The smell of burning choked their lungs.

'At last,' whispered Sal. 'Red Tongue!'

'Ohmygreengreengrass . . . Look at the size of him,' wailed Jaycey.

'And that's only his head,' growled Oxo.

'I can sure smell his stinkin' breath now, innit!' cried Links.

Wills blinked and shook his head. This didn't look like a monster dog to him, but there was no chance to check.

'Your slaughtering days are over, mate!' yelled Oxo. 'One for five and five for Red Tongue!'

'Red Tongue . . . Red Tongue . . . Red Tongue . . .!' they all screamed.

Oxo pawed the ground. 'Wait for it . . .' He lowered his great head. 'Charge!'

The Warriors thundered towards the rocket's nose cone, their heads down, their hearts on fire. Their heads all hit it at once and the cone wobbled slightly.

'And again!' cried Oxo, backing up rapidly, forgetting his earlier experience of falling tail first down a very deep hole. 'Charge!'

The sheep thundered into the nose cone again.

Panic had erupted amongst the humans on the other side of the cone. They came running.

'You said they were dead!' shouted Stanley, as a sheep hurtled past his legs.

'Must I take the blame for everything?' screamed back Holly, racing after the Warriors. 'Just catch them, you stupid egghead!'

But she was on her own.

'One hundred and fifty-three . . .'

Stanley heard the countdown, glanced at his wrist computer and ran back the other way. The rest of the white coats followed his example.

Oxo was in mid-charge when Holly threw herself at him, taking him by surprise. He turned to butt and bite, but she was mad with rage, fury giving her the strength of ten men. She managed to turn him on his back and made for the nose-cone door, dragging the struggling ram with her.

'One hundred and thirty-nine . . .'

'Excellent,' panted Holly, shoving the kicking but near-helpless ram in beside the astronauts' chairs. 'Sheep as well. A perfect ending.'

She turned to back out of the capsule, only to find her perfect ending turning suddenly imperfect: Tod had wriggled half-free of his chair harness. He grabbed her hair, pulling her back inside.

'Abort the take-off!' he shouted. 'Tell them to stop or you're coming with us!'

As she tried to free herself, Holly was aware of the capsule door hissing shut. Beyond, in the control room, the countdown continued despite the sudden unscientific turn of events.

'Professor! Do we abort?' cried the white coats.

Professor Boomberg gazed at the confused pictures being relayed from inside the capsule and shook his head.

'No. Raise the heat shield.'

'But your wife's in there, sir!'

'It's the way she'd have wanted to go . . .' murmured the Professor.

And he couldn't resist a smile.

The other Warriors hadn't seen staple-gun woman throw herself at Oxo. Their heads had been down for the next charge. All they saw was the great ram disappearing into the jaws of the great dog.

'Ohmygrass . . .' wailed Jaycey. 'Red Tongue's eaten Oxo!'

'Nineteen . . . Eighteen . . . Seventeen . . .'

'Another charge . . .' cried Sal. 'For Oxo's sake!'

The Warriors reversed rapidly, then lowered their heads like the fighting machine that they were, and waited for the word from Sal. None of them saw the heat shield, a thick wall of tinted glass, begin to rise out of the floor.

'Charge!' Sal tried to sound like Oxo, proud and strong.

They all crashed painfully into the heat shield.

Inside the capsule, Oxo had squirmed upright. He stared around.

'It's not what I expected a dog's insides to look like,' he muttered.

Then he saw Tod and Ida as well as a yelping Staple Gun Woman, and he gave up thinking. Tod and Ida! It was all too confusing. He leaned sideways and bit Staple Gun Woman's bottom.

'That's for the itchy ear,' he said.

26
Boom

The other Warriors staggered to their hooves, their heads spinning from their collision with the heat shield. Wills looked round and saw Staple Gun Woman's man standing in front of a great bank of computers.

'Seven . . . Six . . . Five . . .'

Wills didn't know why, but he felt sure that when the counting got down to zero, something very bad would happen.

'Charge!' he cried, and raced away from the heat shield.

He was aiming at the white coats now, and one particular pair of dirty trousers. His head made contact, but on his own he wasn't big enough to knock a grown man over.

'You may be smart sheep,' said the trouser-wearer,

with a smug little smile, 'but you're too late. It's Boom Day for Boomberg!'

'Two . . . One . . . Lift off!'

Beyond the tinted heat shield, the rocket that was Red Tongue was already rising. Flames shot from its tail. The noise was deafening. The sheep cowered away, fearful that their fleeces really would scorch in this hottest of all winds.

Inside the capsule, a different noise was bouncing off the walls. Tod had got out of his harness and released Gran, and between them they'd overpowered Holly and forced her into one of the chairs. She was bellowing angrily.

'Let me go!' she yelled. 'And get that smelly creature away from me! It's all his fault!'

Oxo was leaning against her legs, having an exploratory nibble at one of her shoes.

'Not until you tell us where the eject button is!' shouted Gran.

Oxo sat down heavily on Holly's feet and made himself comfortable. This shoe was going to take a bit of concentrated chewing.

'On the wall beside you!' yelled Holly. 'The

red one! Now get him off my feet!'

Tod spun round, saw a large red button and punched it. Instantly, it began to flash. At the same moment, a sign started to flash on the Professor's bank of computer screens.

ASTRONAUT REQUESTS EJECT. CONFIRM: YES OR NO.

'No way . . .' breathed the Professor. 'No way . . .' And he leaned over to press the NO button.

Wills wasn't exactly sure about the word 'eject', but he had an idea it had something to do with throwing things out. Ida used to eject the hens from the barn when she wanted to clean it. Maybe he could get Oxo thrown out of Red Tongue's stomach. He bounced lightly on his toes, in a way that only a lamb can do, then sprang on to the computer control desk.

'Get off!' screamed the Professor.

But Wills lowered his head and managed to smack it into the YES button just before the Professor shoved him angrily aside.

The noise and heat of the rocket launching were fading, and as the tinted heat shield gradually sank back into the floor, the white coats hurried from their computers.

With a snarl at Wills, the Professor followed them. They all peered upwards, shading their eyes, through the open dome of the cavern. The Warriors followed.

'I'm sorry,' said Wills miserably. 'I thought that might work . . . I thought that might save Oxo.'

Sal gave him a little lick. 'Red Tongue's eaten Oxo, dear,' she said. 'We can't get him back.'

The rocket was still rising steadily. It glinted in the blue sky; its heat trail was now a distant flicker. The white coats jumped up and down and cheered. They queued up to shake the Professor's hand. He looked relieved. He looked elated.

Then suddenly, as the sheep stared, they saw Red Tongue's head fall off. The whole head separated from the body and began to float back to earth under what Wills hastily told them was a parachute. The white coats had seen it too. They stopped cheering. A deadly hush fell over the launch site. Everyone's eyes were fixed.

Then it happened. The rest of the rocket turned sharply sideways. It zigzagged wildly across the cloudless blue sky before spiralling downwards to earth. The Warriors all felt the impact as Red Tongue, minus its head, crashed with an almighty explosion somewhere out in the desert.

Professor Boomberg finally broke the stunned silence.

'Open the gate,' he ordered in a flat voice.

As the white coats scurried off, he looked down at the sheep for a moment or two and shook his head.

'If only I'd insisted on rats . . .' he murmured.

The Warriors stood in shocked silence until the humans had gone. Then Links spoke.

'Red Tongue's finished, innit,' he said. 'Butted right out of sheepdom.'

'Ohmygrass,' said Jaycey. 'Wediditwediditwedidit . . .'

'The Songs of the Fleece are never wrong!' cried Sal.

They quickly trotted after the Professor, through the great man-made cavern and out of a sliding steel door that had opened in the hillside. The smoking ruins of Red Tongue's body lay in the distance. But much closer, and still floating gently down beneath its parachute, was the evil dog's head.

As the capsule hit the ground, Holly's seat jolted

forward and smashed into Oxo, who was still sitting on her feet, chewing a nicely softened shoe. His head cracked against the capsule wall. Then Holly's harness sprang open. So did the door. Holly scrambled to her feet, leaving her shoes behind. She trod on Oxo's limp body and, barging past Tod and Gran, leapt out of the capsule – straight into a patch of very prickly pears. She hopped away on her bare feet, pushing aside the Warriors as they ploughed past in the opposite direction.

Links scrabbled up into the capsule and the others squeezed in behind him. Tod and Ida were standing there, gazing down at Oxo. His eyes were shut and he lay perfectly still. The sheep gave Tod and Ida a nod as they edged through to their fallen friend.

It was as the sheep had expected. Links poked Oxo with his nose.

'He's dead, innit,' he announced.

Sal choked back her tears.

'He was a Warrior,' she sobbed. 'An example to us all. A sheep among sheep . . .'

'Ohmygrass . . .' wailed Jaycey. 'I shall miss him sooooo much.'

Wills nodded sadly. 'He was a brave guy. He deserves a medal.'

'What's one of them?' asked Oxo, opening one eye. 'Can you eat it?'

Outside the capsule, the police and the fire service were arriving. In fact, a whole line of official vehicles was bouncing importantly across the desert with sirens blaring.

Sheriff Tiny had been in the first police car, but was on horseback now. He'd seen Lightning wandering out of the hillside and baled out to fetch him. Then he'd spotted the woman who'd stolen Lightning, hopping away through the prickly pears. He swung his lasso and it dropped and tightened around her shoulders in a very satisfying way.

'Just a few questions, ma'am, if you don't mind,' called Tiny, reeling her in. 'I never did catch your name.'

The woman straightened up and regarded him defiantly.

'I am Holly Boomberg,' she declared, 'and my middle name is Petunia.'

She turned and pointed at the skinny, pale-faced man

who was attempting to creep back into the hillside.

'And *that* is my husband, Professor Stanley Boomberg. The *worst scientist* in the universe!'

Sheriff Tiny felt a tug on his boot. The little old lady who'd broken out of Gunslinger City jail was standing beside his horse.

'I did tell you,' she said. 'He's Rhubarb. And those . . .' she pointed proudly at five sheep standing just outside the capsule, '. . . are the Eppingham Rare Breeds.'

27
The Final Rap

The town of Aries End had a proper airport, with departure screens and marble floors and a VIP lounge. Sheriff Tiny made sure the entire Eppingham posse, as he smilingly called them, got to use the lounge when he saw them off next day. He even arranged a tray of cabbage leaves just for the sheep. And he gave Ida back her bag, which she'd left behind during the jail break. Gunslinger City was now full of Boombergs and white coats awaiting trial on a charge of sheepnapping and exploding a space rocket in a public place.

Ida prised the silver stud from Sal's ear and dusted the remains of the glitter from Jaycey's fleece.

'There . . .' she said, patting them both. 'Good girls.'

It still seemed remarkable to Wills that Tod and Ida had come all this way to help. Perhaps there was something about it in the Songs of the Fleece. As he pondered, he was distracted by a familiar chant in the Departures Hall.

'Aries, Aries . . . Rams, Ewes and Lambs!'

'Listen, guys,' said Wills. 'That sounds like Phoenix and Cameron.'

The chanting came closer and, trotting out into the Hall, the sheep saw a crowd of people wearing black-and-white T-shirts and waving flags. On every flag was a picture of a ram's head.

'It is them, innit,' said Links. 'Look, right in the middle of that lot.'

At that moment, Cameron spotted the sheep.

'Hey, Phee! Look! Our sheep! Mom, Mom, come and check this out! Our sheep! The guys who saved our stupid hides out in the desert!'

Tod and Ida didn't want the flock out of their sight for a moment, and hurried anxiously after them. They were astonished to see two teenage boys on their knees with their arms around Oxo and Sal, and a crowd of others stroking and patting the whole flock.

'Thank you, thank you . . .' cried the woman who

was evidently Mom, kissing each of the sheep in turn. 'Cameron, Phoenix, stay there; I have to take a team picture!'

The boys did as they were told, crouching beside the sheep, while Mom got out her camera.

'We finally beat Red Tongue, guys,' said Cameron.

'Whupped 'em out of sight here, at Aries End, just yesterday!' said Phoenix, punching the air.

'What they sayin'?' asked Links.

'They know that Red Tongue got whupped,' said Wills.

He raised a hoof and so did the other Warriors, and Phoenix and Cameron gave them high fives all round.

Mom and the rest of the football fans cheered. And Tod and Ida just stared.

BING BONG . . . a loudspeaker message filled the Hall.

'Will all passengers for London Gatwick please proceed to Gate Five, where Flight RBW One is ready for boarding.'

'Time to go,' translated Wills.

'Better say goodbye then, man,' said Links, and he shook his floppy curls and tapped a hoof as the Warrior Sheep got into line beside him.

'Some humans think us sheep ain't bright
But it seems you guys have seen the light.
And though we never came lookin' for fame,
It's cool that you'll remember our name.
The Songs of the Fleece told us what to do,
And we had a little help from some humans too.
So now ole Red Tongue won't slaughter no more,
Cos the Warrior Sheep has blown him out the door!'

They were rapping towards the Departure Gate now.
The crowd loved the noise.

'More, more!' they shouted, walking with the sheep.
'We'd love to visit the desert again,
But now it's time for some Eppingham rain.
We had a ball in the U S of A,
So goodbye, folks. And have a nice day!'

Christopher Russell was a postman when he had his first radio play broadcast in 1975, having given up a job in the civil service to do shift work and have more daytime hours for writing. Since 1980, he has been a full-time television and radio script writer, and, more recently, a children's novelist. His wife Christine has always been closely involved with his work, storylining and script editing, and has television credits of her own. THE QUEST OF THE WARRIOR SHEEP was the first book they wrote together.

Have you read the first book?

All is quiet on Eppingham Farm. The sheep
that live there chew cud and cauliflower.
Sometimes they butt fence posts.

Until one day a silvery object falls on their
heads. Sal, the Southdown Ewe, knows their
great Sheep God must be in danger.
'Only we can save him!' she cries.

And so the quest of the
Warrior Sheep begins!